"Grant and Applegate are beloved for a reason: They put strong stories at the heart of what they do. *Eve & Adam* . . . is delivered with absolute confidence and a style that SWEEPS YOU ALONG."
—*The New York Times*

"Observant, smart, and unencumbered by emotion, this is a tasty read that readers will DEVOUR IN A FLASH."—*Publishers Weekly*

"This book has so much personality. Every word that comes off the page is some kind of HILARIOUS WIT, humor, or sarcasm, and I absolutely *loved* it!"
—Nosegraze Blog

"Together with a cast of CLEVER and fascinating characters *Eve & Adam* is a great story I can recommend to everyone who loves action, GENETICS, and a thrilling plot!"
—Bewitched Bookworms

"With WITTY banter, lots of action, and plenty of plot TWISTS, *Eve & Adam* was one of the most entertaining books I've read in a long time."—ReadingTeen

EVƎ & ADAM

EVƎ & AↃAM

MICHAEL GRANT AND
KATHERINE APPLEGATE

SQUARE
FISH

FEIWEL AND FRIENDS
New York

SQUARE
FISH

An Imprint of Macmillan
175 Fifth Avenue
New York, NY 10010
macteenbooks.com

Square Fish and the Square Fish logo are trademarks of Macmillan and
are used by Feiwel and Friends under license from Macmillan.

Square Fish books may be purchased for business or promotional use.
For information on bulk purchases, please contact the Macmillan
Corporate and Premium Sales Department at (800) 221-7945 x 5442 or
by e-mail at specialmarkets@macmillan.com.

Library of Congress Cataloging-in-Publication Data Available
ISBN 978-1-250-03419-9 (paperback) / ISBN 978-1-250-02648-4 (e-book)

Originally published in the United States by Feiwel and Friends
First Square Fish Edition: September 2013
Book designed by Ashley Halsey
Square Fish logo designed by Filomena Tuosto

10 9 8 7 6 5 4 3 2 1

AR: 8.0 / LEXILE: HL560L

for
Jean Feiwel

friend
visionary
responsible party

EV3

I AM THINKING OF AN APPLE WHEN THE STREETCAR HITS AND MY LEG SEVERS and my ribs crumble and my arm is no longer an arm but something unrecognizable, wet and red.

An apple. It was in a vendor's stall at the farmers' market off Powell. I'd noticed it because it was so weirdly out of place, a defiant crimson McIntosh in an army of dull green Granny Smiths.

When you die—and I realize this as I hurtle through the air like a wounded bird—you should be thinking about love. If not love, at the very least you should be counting up your sins or wondering why you didn't cross at the light.

But you should not be thinking about an apple.

I register the brakes screeching and the horrified cries before I hit the pavement. I listen as my bones splinter and shatter. It's not an unpleasant sound, more delicate than I would have imagined. It reminds me of the bamboo wind chimes on our patio.

A thicket of legs encircles me. Between a bike messenger's ropy calves I can just make out the 30% OFF TODAY ONLY sign at Lady Foot Locker.

I should be thinking about love right now—not apples, and certainly not a new pair of Nikes—and then I stop thinking altogether because I am too busy screaming.

• • •

I OPEN MY EYES AND THE LIGHT IS BLINDING. I KNOW I MUST BE dead because in the movies there's always a tunnel of brilliant light before someone croaks.

"Evening? Stay with us, girl. Evening? Cool name. Look at me, Evening. You're in the hospital. Who should we call?"

The pain slams me down, and I realize I'm not dead after all, although I really wish I could be because maybe then I could breathe instead of scream.

"Evening? You go by Eve or Evening?"

Something white smeared in red hovers above me like a cloud at sunset. It pokes and prods and mutters. There's another, then another. They are grim but determined, these clouds. They talk in fragments. Pieces, like I am in pieces. *Vitals. Prep. Notify. Permission. Bad.*

"Evening? Who should we call?"

"Check her phone. Who's got her damn cell?"

"They couldn't find it. Just her school ID."

"What's your mom's name, hon? Or your dad's?"

2

"My dad is dead," I say, but it comes out in ear-splitting moans, a song I didn't know I could sing. It's funny, really, because I cannot remotely carry a tune. A C+ in Beginning Women's Chorus—and that was totally a pity grade—but here I am, singing my heart out.

Dead would be so good right now. My dad and me, just us, not this.

OR 2's ready. No time. Now now now.

I'm pinned flat like a lab specimen, and yet I'm moving, flying past the red and white clouds. I didn't know I could fly. So many things I know this afternoon that I didn't know this morning.

"Evening? Eve? Give me a name, hon."

I try to go back to the morning, before I knew that clouds could talk, before I knew a stranger could retrieve the dripping stump of your own leg.

What do I do with it? he'd asked.

"My mother's Terra Spiker," I sing.

The clouds are silent for a moment, and then I fly from the room of bright light.

I AWAKEN TO AN ARGUMENT. THE MAN IS SIMMERING, THE WOMAN ON FULL BOIL.

They're out of my view, behind an ugly green curtain. I try to do what I always do when my parents fight, adjust my earbuds and crank the volume to brain-numb, but something is wrong. My right arm is not obeying me, and when I touch my ear with my left hand, I discover a thick gauze headband. I've sprouted long tubes from my arms and my nose.

"She's my daughter," the woman says, "and if I say she's leaving, she's leaving."

"Please, listen to me. She's going to be your one-legged daughter if you take her out of here."

The man is pleading, and I realize he's not my dad because (a) my dad was never a pleader—more of a pouter, really; and (b) he's dead.

"I have superior facilities, the best medical staff money can buy." The woman punctuates this with a dramatic exhalation. It's my mother's trademark sigh.

"She's in critical condition in the ICU after a fourteen-hour surgery. There's every chance she's going to lose that leg, and you want to *move* her? Because . . . what? It's more convenient? Your sheets have a higher thread count? What exactly?"

I feel pretty okay, sort of floaty and disconnected, but this man, who I've decided must be a doctor, sounds a little freaked out about my leg, which, as it happens, doesn't seem to be behaving any better than my arm.

I should probably reassure him, get my mother off his case—when she's like this it's best to retreat and regroup—but the tube stuck down my throat makes that impossible.

"I will not release this patient," the doctor says, "under any circumstances."

Silence. My mother is the god of painful pauses.

"Do you know," she finally asks, "what the new hospital wing is called, Doctor?"

More silence. The contraptions I'm tethered to chirp contentedly.

"That would be the Spiker Neurogenetics Pavilion," the doctor finally says, and suddenly he sounds defeated, or maybe he's missing his tee time.

"I have an ambulance waiting outside," my mother says. Check and mate. "I trust you'll expedite the paperwork."

"She dies, it's on you."

His choice of words must bother me, because my machines start blaring like a cheap car alarm.

"Evening?" My mother rushes to my side. Tiffany earrings, Bulgari perfume, Chanel suit. Mommy, Casual Friday edition.

"Sweetheart, it's going to be okay," she says. "I've got everything under control."

The quaver in her voice betrays her. My mother does not quaver.

I try to move my head a millimeter and realize maybe I'm not feeling so okay after all. Also, my car alarm won't shut up. The doctor is muttering about my leg, or what's left of my leg, and my mother is burying her head into my pillow, her lacquered nails digging into my shoulder. She may actually be crying.

I am pretty sure we're all losing it, and then, on my other shoulder, I feel a firm pressure.

It's a hand.

I follow the path from hand to arm to neck to head, moving just my eyes this time.

The hand is connected to a guy.

"Dr. Spiker," he says, "I'll get her into the ambulance."

My mother sniffles into my gown. She rouses herself, stands erect. She is Back in Control.

"What the hell are you doing here, Solo?" she snaps.

"You left your phone and briefcase behind when you got the call about the"—he jerks his chin toward me—"the accident. I followed in one of the Spiker limos."

I don't recognize this guy or, for that matter, his name—because, really, what kind of a name is Solo, anyway?—but he must work for my mother.

He looks down at me, past the tubes and the panic. He is scruffy-looking with too much hair, too little shaving. He's tall and wide-shouldered, muscular, blondish. Extremely blue eyes. My preliminary taxonomy: skater or surfer, one of those guys.

I'd really like him to get his hand off me because he doesn't know me and I'm already having personal-space issues, what with the tubes and the IV.

"Chill, Eve," he tells me, which I find annoying. The first phrase that comes to mind involves the word "off," preceded by a word I have absolutely no chance of pronouncing since it includes the letter "F."

Not in the mood to meet new friends.

In the mood for more painkillers.

Also, my mother calls me Evening and my friends call me E.V. But nobody calls me Eve. So there's that, too.

"Please reconsider, Dr. Spiker . . ." The doctor trails off.

"Let's get this show on the road," says the guy named Solo. He's about my age, a junior, maybe a senior. If he does work for my mother, he's either an intern or a prodigy. "Will you be coming in the ambulance, Dr. Spiker?"

"No. God knows what microorganisms are in that ambulance. My driver's waiting," my mother says. "I'll need to make some calls and I doubt the back of an ambulance is the place. I'll meet you at the lab."

The doctor sighs. He flips a switch and my contraptions still.

My mother kisses my temple. "I'll get everything set up. Don't worry about a thing."

I blink to show that I am not, in fact, worried about a thing. Not with the morphine drip taking the edge off.

Solo hands my mother her briefcase and phone. She vanishes, but I can hear the urgent staccato of her Jimmy Choos.

"Bitch," the doctor says when she's out of earshot. "I don't like this at all."

"No worries," Solo says.

No worries. Yeah, not for you, genius. Go away. Stop talking to me or about me. And take your hand off me, I'm nauseous.

The doctor checks one of my IV bags. "Uh-huh," he mutters. "You an MD?"

Solo makes a half smile. It's knowing and a little smug. "Just a gofer, Doctor."

Solo gathers up my bagged belongings and my backpack. Suddenly I remember I have AP Bio homework. A worksheet on Mendel's First Law. *When a pair of organisms reproduce sexually, their offspring randomly inherit one of the two alleles from each parent.*

Genetics. I like genetics, the rules, the order. My best friend, Aislin, says it's because I'm a control freak. Like mother, like daughter.

I have a load of homework, I want to say, but everyone's buzzing about purposefully. It occurs to me my biology worksheet won't be all that relevant if I'm dying.

I believe death is on the list of acceptable excuses for missing homework.

"You're going to be fine," Solo tells me. "Running 10Ks in no time."

I try to speak. "Unh onh," I say.

Yep. Can't pronounce "F" with a tube in your mouth.

Then it occurs to me: How does he know I like to run?

– 3 –

SOLO

So. This is the boss's daughter.

I'd seen pictures of her, of course. You can't go into Terra Spiker's office and not see photos of her daughter. My favorite's this one where Eve's crossing a finish line, all sweaty and flushed, with a killer smile on her face.

I glance down at the stretcher. Eve's got a serious bruise coming up under both eyes. Still, you can see the resemblance to her mom. High cheekbones, big, deep-set eyes. Tall, slender.

That's about it for similarities, though. Terra's a total ice queen bitch: frosty blond hair, calculating gray eyes. Eve . . . well, she's different. Her hair is sun-streaked gold, and her eyes are this mellow brown color.

At least I'm pretty sure they're brown.

They're a little wobbly at the moment.

There's not a lot of room on the narrow bench in the back of the ambulance. I nearly go flying when they pull away from the emergency room and crank on the siren.

I grin. "Floor it, dude," I yell to the driver.

The doctor sitting on the other side of Eve's stretcher sends me a *what the hell?* scowl.

I know it seems wrong to enjoy this, but still: the siren and the zooming through the streets of San Francisco while all the other cars scatter? Very cool.

Besides, Eve's going to be fine.

I think.

We're at the bridge in no time. *The* bridge. The Golden Gate, still the best, never get tired of it. I fantasize sometimes how great it would be to ride a longboard down the cable. Yes, there would almost certainly be a long plunge to a hideous death. But before that it would be amazing.

I sit with my elbows on my knees, trying to hunch my shoulders forward a little. I have good shoulders, might as well reveal them. I know she's checking me out. Fair enough, because I'm checking her out.

"Ah ahhh ahhhh!"

Eve cries out suddenly. She's in pain. Bad pain. So it's possible she's not really checking me out.

"Doc," I say, "can't you help the girl out?"

He leans over to check the IV tube. It's gotten kinked, the flow cut off. He straightens it and tears off strips of white tape to hold it in place.

"She'll be better in a second."

"Cool," I say. I lean in close so she can hear me. "I got him to crank up the morphine," I say, speaking loud and slow.

Her eyeballs kind of roll toward me. She doesn't seem to be focusing very well. And for a second I think, whoa, what if I'm wrong? What if she actually dies?

All of a sudden it's like I want to cry. Not happening, obviously—crying, I mean—but there's just this sudden wave of sadness.

I shake it off as well as I can. But once you start seeing the Big D, the Reaper, sitting beside you, it's very hard to stop.

"Don't die, okay?" I say.

Her confused eyeballs are looking for me. Like I'm a target and she can't quite line up the sights.

So I get close again and I kind of touch her face and aim her head at me. Unfortunately, I lean my other hand on her leg—the wrong one—and there's some yelling from Eve and from the doctor.

Which makes it impossible for me to say what I had planned to say to reassure her: *Don't worry. I've seen things. I know things.*

Your mom has powers.

She won't let you die.

EVƎ

Operation? What operation?

They tell me it lasted fourteen hours.

I wasn't really there. I was in a weird landscape of dreams, nightmares, and memories—with a little shopping thrown in.

I'm pretty sure I had an extended dream where Aislin and I wandered around the big Westfield Mall downtown on Market Street. Of course, it could have been a memory. It's hard to keep track of the difference when your blood flows with whatever drug they use to separate your consciousness from your senses.

My new doctor, the one who arrived with the private ambulance, has on a lab coat that reads:

Dr. Anderson
Spiker Biopharmaceuticals
Creating Better Lives

It's a chic low-sheen black. He looks like he should be foiling my hair, not checking my pulse.

Solo keeps staring at me. Not a *she's dead meat* stare. More like he's an anthropologist who's just discovered a new tribe deep in the heart of the Amazon.

The road was a little bumpy over the bridge, but I've discovered I can surf the pain, feel it roll and crest and crash. If you think about something, anything, else, it's not so bad.

The fact that I can think at all, when my leg has recently been—well, chopped off and glued back on is, I believe, the medical term—is kind of a miracle, and I'm grateful for the random thoughts that flood my brain.

Things I Think About, Exhibit A:

How I got a B+ on my oral report in bio, which sucks because it's going to bring my grade down, and possibly my GPA, which means I won't get into a decent college, which means I'll never escape the clutches of my crazy-ass mother, and I know this really doesn't matter in the grand scheme of things, especially now, but that's not the point, is it?

I'm pretty sure Ms. Montoya dropped my grade because of my intro: "Boys have nipples." Perhaps this was news to her.

It was a risky ploy, sure, but when it's second period and you're the first speaker and the Red Bull has only ignited a handful of brain cells, you do what you have to do.

There were twenty kids in the room. When I moved to the

front to tie my iPad to the projector, I'd say I had a total of eight eyeballs out of a possible forty watching me.

I delivered my opening line, and thirty-nine eyeballs were trained on me. Jennifer has one lazy eye, so I was never going to get all forty.

"Why?" I asked. I cued the first slide, which was of a boy's chest. It was a fine chest, a very fine chest, and I knew it would hold the attention of the nine straight girls and one gay boy.

It was a cheap ploy, but sex sells. It always has, it always will, and in the context of a boring report day in my boring eleventh-grade biology class at boring Bay Area School of Arts and Sciences, a smooth, hard chest over rippled abs was just the ticket.

The way I had the presentation laid out, we'd see that slide two more times. We'd also see DNA molecules, a little video snippet of dinosaurs demonstrating the concept of survival of the fittest—because seriously, there's no bad time to show bored kids some dinosaur-on-dinosaur violence—and the inevitable graphs, pie charts, and equations that would earn me a decent grade. And chest to keep my audience.

I thought I had the thing aced.

Wrong.

So, okay, I phoned it in a little. But still. A B+ after *those* abs?

Things I Think About, Exhibit B:

How I was supposed to bail out Aislin's dirtbag boyfriend after school, which is why I was checking her latest frantic text when that out-of-place apple caught my eye, which is why I wasn't looking where I was going, which is why I am now in an ambulance with an MD from Aveda and some guy with a perpetually smug look on his face.

Things I Think About, Exhibit C:

How I missed prom yet again. (I had a previous engagement, organizing my sock drawer while watching old Jon Stewarts on my laptop.) Aislin claims I didn't miss anything: It was a total waste of a good buzz. Even with the purse searches and rent-a-cops, she managed to sneak in three separate flasks of lemon vodka.

I am a little worried about Aislin.

Things I Think About, Exhibit D:

How I can't figure out the deal with this Solo guy. Is my mother using him as her stand-in? Is that his job?

Things I Think About, Exhibit E:

How Solo's eyes have this distant, *don't mess with me* edge to them. They'd be hard to sketch, but then, I can never get faces right.

Last week during Life Drawing, Ms. Franklin asked me if I'd ever considered majoring in art instead of biology.

I asked her for a new eraser.

Things I Think About, Exhibit F:

How Solo smells like the ocean when he leans close and smooths my hair.

Things I Think About, Exhibit G:

How Solo, once he's done gently smoothing my hair, starts pounding out an incredibly inept drum solo on my oxygen tank.

Things I Think About, Exhibit H:

How I might never run again.

— 5 —

SOLO

We pull into Spiker Biopharm. It's located on the back side of the Tiburon peninsula across the Golden Gate and down some windy roads. As you drive up it's not mind-boggling or anything, because the road at that point is maybe two hundred feet up above the ocean, and the Spiker complex is more vertical than horizontal. It spreads down that steep slope from the road above to the water below. And it is big. From the water, it looks like the City of Oz had a giant baby with one of those big-city Apple stores.

The place is built around three massive spikes—as in Spiker, heh—with each of the spikes being an elevator array. Connecting them is a sort of ziggurat construction with terraces, open spaces, entire floors given over to gardens, sandy volleyball courts, a pool.

It is, without question, a great place to work. If you can get past some of the people.

And number one among the people you have to get past is the boss woman herself, Terra Spiker. Known throughout the campus as Terror Spiker.

That, to me, is a major clue someone should have gotten: If you're going to name your daughter Terra, and if she's going to grow up to be a psycho-bitch, people are going to start calling her "Terror."

The way the complex is laid out, the floors are bigger below and smaller above. The bottom floor, Level One, is the largest space, the Orphan Disease Research Division. They focus on the many less-than-popular diseases that no one is ever going to get rich curing.

Whatever else you can say about Terra, she's done some very major work down there on Level One. As in cures. As in people who were being eaten alive by some parasite or some germ are walking around alive today because of Level One. Because Terra Spiker said, "Screw profits, we're throwing a billion dollars into beating this disease."

The reason no one gets serious about investigating Spiker Biopharm? Because of what happens down there on Level One, that's why. Because the psycho-bitch saves a bunch of lives.

On the other hand, the reason so many people think about investigating Spiker? Because of what happens on Levels Seven and Eight.

Me, I live on Level Four. My parents, Isabel and Jeffrey Plissken, were Terra's business partners way back in the day, when all they had was a broken-down IBM, some petri dishes, and a dream.

I don't remember them. It's like that.

I could say Terra raised me, but that would be wrong. She's no mother to me. She gives me a place to live, an education, a job at the lab.

She tolerates me.

She wouldn't even do that if she knew.

EVƎ

A STEEL DOOR OPENS AND WE ENTER AN OVERLIT GARAGE. TWO MEN AND A WOMAN, clad in black lab coats like Dr. Anderson's, are waiting for me. I have an entourage.

"She's stable," Dr. Anderson remarks, "doing well," and the other three lab coats seem surprised. They mutter medically in ways I can't decipher.

I am whisked into a long white-tiled tunnel. Solo keeps pace beside me.

We arrive at a large glass elevator. Each member of the group stands before a wall-mounted lens.

"Optical scanner," Solo explains as a green light clears him.

I've only been to my mother's office a couple times. (She says mixing home and work is like mixing a single malt with Sprite.) The complex is visually stunning, or at least that's what *Architectural Digest* said: "Frank Gehry on steroids." When you look at satellite photos, you see more security than the Pentagon. Even the security gates have security gates.

It's the kind of sprawling building you'd expect to find in Silicon Valley, not Marin. But Spiker Biopharm is a different kind of company, my mother likes to say, and I suppose that's why she decided to locate it in a different kind of place.

"Different" would be her word, but others have had worse things to say. As drug companies go, Spiker's the bad boy on the Harley your dad doesn't want you to date. I first realized this in fifth grade, when Ms. Zagarenski passed out a form letter soliciting parents to give classroom talks for Career Week. She sent a note home with everybody but me ("Your mother's so busy, dear") and I got the clue. Even Danny Rappaport got one, and we all knew his dad ran the largest pot farm in Mendocino.

The elevator shoots to the sixth floor. The doors open to reveal a breathtaking lobby. Marble, glass, steel, tiered fountain. It looks like the Ritz-Carlton my dad used to retreat to when the fights dragged on too long.

I'm wondering when the concierge will show up, and suddenly here she is.

"Baby," says my mother, "welcome to my world." Burying me in her perfumed embrace, she lowers her voice to a whisper and adds: "Mommy's going to fix everything."

She leads the way through swinging doors, and suddenly we are in a hospital.

A really swank hospital.

Dr. Anderson has a platoon of assistants: specialists, nurses, techs, but, as far as I can tell, only one patient. They are shocked at how well I am doing. Everyone wants to have a look at my mangled arm, swollen like an overcooked hot dog. I learn that my spleen, whatever that is, has been ruptured. Also, I've lost a rib.

"You'll never miss it," Dr. Anderson assures me.

The star attraction, however, is my reattached leg with its Frankenstein stitches. My mother is especially interested—my mother, who always made my dad apply Band-Aids because the sight of blood made her woozy.

My gown is an oversized napkin, barely covering the essentials. I'd be massively embarrassed if I weren't so drugged up. Fortunately, Solo seems to have stayed behind in the hall.

"Miraculous," breathes a nurse.

It looks horrifying to me, all the blood and goo and gauze, but I have to admit I'm not feeling as awful as I was a few hours ago. The pain has gone from blinding to merely throbbing. And when they finally remove the tube from my throat, the first thing I say is "I'm hungry" in a hoarse whisper, which gives rise to appreciative laughter and applause.

One of the nurses, an older guy with a trim gray beard, introduces me to my room appointments like a bellboy sniffing for a tip. Wi-Fi! Flat-screen! Italian marble! Heated towel rack!

"Is there anything you need?" my mother asks. "I'm having your pajamas and robe picked up from the house."

I try to focus. "My laptop. My *Titus Andronicus* T-shirt, you know, the blue one? Maybe some Clearasil."

"You won't be needing your laptop any time soon."

"Do you know where my phone is?" I croak. "I should call Aislin. I think that guy—Solo?—I think he said somebody turned it in."

A tight smile. My mother does not like Aislin. She tolerates her the way she tolerated the pet ferret I could never quite house-break. I believe this is because Aislin shorted out our seven-thousand-dollar full-body Swedish massage chair with a puked-up Mojito, but Aislin is convinced the tide turned when she suggested a cure for my mother's chronic headaches. I gather that the phrase "get some" may have been employed.

"Derek, see if Solo has my daughter's phone." A tech scurries away, and moments later Solo appears, carrying a plastic bag.

"Someone turned in your cell," he says. "Also your sketch-book. It's a little muddy. Nothing too major, though."

"Thanks," I say. I sound like my great-grandmother after her nightly Marlboro menthol.

"I'll take that," my mother says, but for some reason, Solo refuses to let go of my sketchbook. She yanks and it falls to the floor.

When Solo retrieves the pad, it's open to a sketch I've been working on for several weeks for Life Drawing. We're supposed to draw a person, either from memory or from our imagination, without referring to a model or a photo.

Easy, I thought.

Turns out: not so easy.

Solo stares at the drawing. It started out as a guy's face in profile. Not a memory, just something that came to me. Mostly it's just lines, angles, planes. A preschool Picasso.

It's deeply lame.

Solo takes it in, meets my eyes.

"Interesting," my mother says without looking. She snaps the sketchbook shut and hands it to an assistant.

My mother doesn't like art, mine or anybody else's, probably because my dad was an artist. "Austin was a failed sculptor," she's fond of saying—she always pauses a beat here, raising a professionally waxed brow—"but he was an accomplished failure."

"So you're an artist," Solo says.

"She's a patient," my mother answers, "and she needs to rest."

"Right." Solo starts to hand her my phone.

"No," I say quickly. "Would you check for messages first? The password's 0123."

"Impenetrable." Solo scans my mail. "Aislin wants to know 'WTF are you dead or what OMG please please please call.'"

"Didn't you call her?" I ask my mother. "She must be so—"

"I've been a little busy, dear," my mother says crisply. "I'll have someone give her a call, let her know you're all right."

I can tell she's planning to forget to remember. "Would you do it?" I ask Solo. I don't know why him exactly, except that he's still holding my phone.

"Sure. No problem." He taps the screen. "Got it. Don't worry. I have a photographic memory."

"Really?" I ask vaguely. Suddenly I am incredibly weary.

"Just for things that matter," Solo replies.

His gaze lingers on my leg, then moves on to my middle. I am not sure if he's staring at my flattened arm or my boobs (also pretty flat), but either way, I'm not dressed for company.

He meets my eyes for just a moment. Then he hands my mother my cell and makes his way past my bedside fan club.

I WAKE UP HOURS LATER, CLAWING MY WAY OUT OF THE VICODIN HAZE. IT'S DARK, but my room is lit with soft yellow light. If I squint just right, I could be in a romantic restaurant. On a really bad date.

The first thing I see is Solo, looking with intense focus at the iPad they use in lieu of an old-fashioned clipboard medical chart. It's not the concentration of someone trying to make sense of something he doesn't understand. It's the concentration of a guy confirming something he's already suspected.

He hears me moving. The iPad is back in the slot at the foot of my bed and he's smiling at me. Covering up. Looking innocent.

I think: *Strange boy I really don't know, don't you realize nothing is more suspicious than an innocent look?*

Before I can say anything, Solo slips out the door. Seconds later, a nurse arrives. I haven't seen her before, so I figure she must be part of the evening shift.

I close my eyes, pretending to sleep. I'm not in the mood to chat.

She checks the bandage on my leg. It's one hell of a bandage.

Gently she begins to cut away the tape and gauze and pressure mesh. It doesn't hurt, but it doesn't make me happy, either.

"Oh my God!" she says.

She has laid the flesh bare and her first thought is to call up a deity.

I risk a slit eye to see what horror she's witnessed.

She's not looking at my face. She's staring down at my leg. And she's not horrified, exactly.

She's amazed. She's moved. She's seeing something she never expected to see and can't quite believe is real.

I'm afraid to look, because I know that something must be very wrong.

Or, just possibly, very right.

SOLO

THE SPIKER COMPLEX HAS AN AMAZING GYM. EVERYONE IS CONSTANTLY NAGGED TO stay in shape. I don't need to be nagged and I don't need to be coached. I need to be left alone.

I run on the inside track. I run barefoot; I prefer it. The soles of my feet make a different sound, nothing like those three-hundred-dollar running shoes, groaning as all that shock-absorbing rubber takes the impact. My feet are almost silent.

I run and then I hit the weights, the crunches, all that. I like weights—they're specific. There's no bull in weight lifting; you either get that seventy-pound dumbbell up to your chest or you don't. Yes or no, no kind-of.

After weights I go into the dark, smelly side room where the speed bags and heavy bags are. The rest of the massive gym complex is spotless and bright and gazed-down-upon by screens.

The boxing room—well, there's just something seedy about the sport that comes through, even if the designer you hired insisted on a lovely shade of teal for the ring ropes.

Pete's there, all ready to go.

Sometimes I go rounds with Pete. Pete's older than me, maybe twenty-five. I've never asked. But he's one of the geeks so we tend to get along well. We speak geek, or we would if we didn't have slobbery mouthpieces in and weren't beating on each other.

Pete's not as quick as I am, and he looks softer and spongier than I do. But damn, when he connects you know you've been hit. You know it and you have to acknowledge it as your brain spins inside its bone cradle trying to reconnect all the switches.

I kind of love it.

It's obviously crazy that I enjoy getting punched. But I do. You take a hard one to the side of your head, a shot that makes you feel as if you aren't wearing sparring headgear at all, one that rings the bells in your ear, and then you come back from it, still swinging? To me that's one of life's finest moments.

Hit me. No, I mean hit me hard. Turn my knees to overcooked linguine.

And I take it and come back with a combination? Prodigious.

I'm done and covered in sweat. From the hair on my head down to my feet, wet, shiny, panting, grinning, wondering if I'm going to get feeling back in the left side of my face.

"Wimp," Pete says.

"Weakling," I respond.

"I don't feel right beating up on a little girl."

"Don't feel bad, Pete. Keep at it and you may learn to throw a punch that actually connects some day."

With our ritual abuse concluded, we make an appointment for the day after tomorrow. Pete heads for the gym's showers; I head for my quarters.

My quarters, my place, my space. It's on Level Four, where Spiker maintains rooms for visiting scientists and dignitaries. Some of those rooms are amazing. My quarters do not justify the word "amazing," but they aren't bad.

In any case, this place is a major improvement over the boarding school in Montana that Terra shipped me off to after my parents died. Some kind of tough-love dude-ranch high school for troubled kids called Distant Drummer Academy. I wasn't troubled—unless you count being orphaned overnight—and I wasn't in high school, but Terra provided them with a nice diagnosis of severe ODD. And a hefty donation.

Oppositional Defiant Disorder? Yeah, I can do that.

I lasted eight days.

After they kicked me out, Terra gave me two options: I could live at her place, or I could live at Spiker.

We both knew which one I'd choose.

I have a single room, but it's big enough for a queen-sized bed and a sofa, TV, desk, beanbag chair, and mini kitchen. Except for the two framed photos on my desk, it's as sterile as a hotel room. I like it that way.

I barely notice the photos anymore. There's one of my parents at a podium, my mom in a shimmering green evening gown, my dad in a tux. They're accepting an award, flashing smiles. And there's one of me and my mom reading a book together. We're in some kind of waiting room, sitting on orange vinyl chairs. I don't remember where it was, or why we were there.

But then, I don't remember much of anything.

Next to the mini kitchen is a small bathroom. That's where I strip down, soap up, and shower off.

That's where I start thinking about the girl.

Like I don't know her name: the girl. Please, Solo. I know her name. Evening. E.V. to her friends.

Eve.

There's a problem with that name, Eve. You say "Eve" and you think Garden of Eden, and then you think of Eve and Adam, naked but tastefully concealed by strategic shrubbery.

Except at this particular moment, my brain is not generating shrubbery.

So, basically, that's despicable. The girl had her leg chopped off. She just got out of surgery. So I add shrubbery.

And yet the shrubbery doesn't stay put. It's moving shrubbery. It's disappearing shrubbery.

Which is deeply wrong of me. I step back under the twin showerheads and blast myself with hot water. Maybe I should make it cold water. But I don't want to.

"That's the problem with you, dude," I say, speaking to myself. "You suck at doing things you don't want to do."

I don't feel bad speaking to myself.

Who else have I got?

Solo isn't just a name, it's a description. I have no actual friends. I have some online ones, but that's not quite the same.

I've never had a girlfriend.

When I touched Eve, she was the first girl I'd touched since coming here to live six years ago. Unless you count women scientists and techs and office workers I've accidentally brushed in the hallways.

Sometimes I do count those. It's a normal human behavior to count whatever you have to count.

"Back up, man," I tell myself softly. "She's a Spiker. She's one of the enemy."

The microphones won't pick up what I say with the shower running. I know these things. Even though I'm not supposed to. For six years I've lived and breathed this place. I know it. I know it all.

And I know what I'm going to do with it.

As soon as Eve is gone.

9

EVƎ

THREE LITTLE DAYS, BUT OH MY GOD, CAN THEY BE LONG.

Time is relative. An hour spent watching paint dry is much longer than an hour getting a massage.

Which is exactly what I'm doing. Getting a massage from Luna, the massage therapist.

Luna doesn't touch The Leg.

In my head, The Leg is capitalized because The Leg is what my whole life seems to be about now. Every single person I've seen in the past few days asks me about The Leg.

How is it?

How's The Leg?

The Leg is attached. Thanks for asking. There's The Leg right there. It's on display, always outside of the sheets and blanket, although the whole thing is still so wrapped up it looks like I borrowed The Leg from some ancient Egyptian mummy.

How's The Leg?

It seems a bit mummyish, thanks.

I had a dream where The Leg was no longer attached. Not a happy dream, that. It scared me. I try to be glib and tough and all SEAL Team Six about it, but in all desperate seriousness: I was scared.

"I need Aislin," I say to my mother.

"Aislin is a drunken slut," she replies, without looking up from her laptop.

This is diplomatic for her.

I decide to change the subject. "What are you working on?"

With effort, she pulls her gaze from the screen. "Fluff. A vanity project for one of the biochems."

"Fluff?"

"Educational software. Project 88715."

"Catchy. The kids'll eat that up."

"Mm-hmm." She returns to her screen.

"Aislin is not a slut," I say. I don't deny the drunken part. "She's been in a steady relationship for months. Anyway, she's my friend. I miss her."

"Talk to the masseuse," my mother says. She glares at Luna. "Who are you? Talk to my daughter."

I feel the tremor go through Luna. Luna is probably fifty years old, a very nice Haitian woman. I like Luna. She doesn't hurt me as much as the various other physical therapists.

Luna has six kids. Two are in college and one is a real estate broker in San Rafael.

Number of things I have in common with Luna? Zero.

"I want my friends," I say.

"Pfff. Friends, plural?" my mother asks. "Since when do you have friends, plural? You have one friend and she's a drunken slut."

"I'm lonely. There aren't even any other patients. The only one around who's my age is Solo."

"You haven't talked to him, have you?" my mother asks, feigning a casual tone. Casual, like warm and fuzzy, is not part of her emotional repertoire.

"No," I lie, wondering why she cares.

Actually, I've seen him every day since my arrival, passing by my room with studied indifference. He only spoke once, to tell me that he called Aislin and told her not to worry about me.

His eyes are disturbingly blue.

Against my better judgment I ask, "Who is Solo, anyway? And why is he here?"

My mother ignores me. She has different Ignore settings, and this one means she's hiding something. She thinks she is inscrutable, and maybe she is, to her minions, but I've had seventeen years to deconstruct her poker face.

Before I can press her to answer, Dr. Anderson strides purposefully into the room. He always strides purposefully, although he doesn't seem to have much purpose, what with me being his sole patient.

"How's the leg?" he asks.

"The Leg is bored," I answer. "The Leg wants to know why it can't go home and recover."

"You've been here three days, Evening! Are you insane?" my mother cries.

"I should leave," Luna says meekly, half-question, half-hope.

"Stay," my mother commands. "Calm her down."

"I don't need to be calmed down. I need Aislin. I need something to *do*."

"You have to take this slowly, Evening," Dr. Anderson intones. He has perfect teeth and the graying temples of a Just For Men model. "This kind of recovery is measured in months, not days."

"I'm missing the end of the school year." I am starting to feel quite sorry for myself. "I have homework, tests. Oh crap, my bio exam is Tuesday! And my Life Drawing project is half my semester grade."

"You can't draw," my mother says. "Your fingers are crushed. Your arm's a mess." She pauses, mentally thumbing through her What Mothers Are Supposed To Know file. "She *is* right-handed, isn't she?" she asks Dr. Anderson.

He nods discreetly.

"At least can I have my laptop? I can type with my left hand."

My mother glances at her own laptop.

She is having an inspiration. You can practically see the giant lightbulb throbbing over her head.

"Evening, I have just the project for you! Something to keep you thoroughly occupied."

"I don't want a project. I want to spend a couple of hours with Aislin. I want you to send a car for her and bring her here."

Luna has moved to my lower back, and seriously, my desire

to fight with my mother—even if it is a respite from boredom—is diminishing with each deep, healing stroke.

"It involves genetics." My mother sets aside her computer and comes to my bedside. "You love genetics. I would even pay you to do it."

"Pay me?"

"Why not? I'd have to pay someone else to test it. What do you want? A hundred dollars? A thousand?"

My mother, ladies and gentlemen: one of America's preeminent businesswomen. Not a clue as to what a dollar is.

"I want ten thousand dollars," I say.

Dr. Anderson nods his approval.

"Is that a good number?" my mother asks. She turns the question over to Luna. "Is that a good number?"

"Ma'am, I don't—"

"Whatever," my mother snaps. She makes a brusque gesture with her hand. "The point is, I have something that will keep you busy."

"Aislin will keep me busy. That's my price: Aislin. You can keep the money."

She taps her freshly tended nails. French manicures, twice a week. Five tiny crescent moons dance on my bed rail.

She sighs.

Dr. Anderson examines a smudge on his stethoscope.

"One visit," my mother says at last. "I'll have security search her. If she has any drugs or booze on her, I'll confiscate them and have security rough her up."

I assume that's bluster.

Then I look at her again, at my mother, and I'm not so sure it is. This is a woman with a billion-dollar company. This building is big enough to house what amounts to a small hospital among many, many other things.

Can my mother actually have people beaten up?

Maybe. Maybe she can.

She smiles to show she doesn't mean it. The smile convinces me that she can.

"So what's the project? You want me to wash some test tubes?"

"No, that's why we have people like Solo," she says. "You're a Spiker."

I feel a slight twinge of sympathy for Solo. I'd been assuming he's some kind of wunderkind, and here she's talking about him as if he were her servant.

People like . . .

Quite a bit of condescension locked up in those two words.

"This will be a wonderful introduction to the kind of thinking and creativity we require at Spiker," my mother says. "It'll challenge you, sweetheart. Bring out the talent I know you have hidden deep, deep down inside you." She's getting excited now. The lines in her forehead seem to smooth; her eyes gaze with a certain wild excitement at the horizon.

She pauses, waiting to be sure she has my undivided attention.

"I want you, Evening, to design the perfect boy."

Luna stops rubbing.

"Am I doing this with crayons? Or will I be working with Play-Doh?"

My mother smiles tolerantly. "Oh, I think we can do a little better than that. You can start tomorrow morning. If you do it, I'll have your little friend here tomorrow afternoon."

"I think Aislin has her dance class on—"

"Evening. When I send for people, they come."

10

"THIS IS WHERE YOU'LL BE WORKING. PLAYING."

My mother hesitates, frowns, realizes she's frowning and that frowning causes lines, and unfrowns. "Play, work, call it whatever you like."

"So long as I do it."

"Exactly."

Solo is pushing my wheelchair while my mother leads the way. At the last minute, the orderly who was supposed to be assisting us this morning had an attack of stomach pains. His backup couldn't be located.

It crosses my mind, just for a nanosecond, that Solo might have arranged to be here with me. Maybe he's as desperate for company as I am.

Solo pushes my wheelchair into a horseshoe-shaped work station. It's an amazing space with soaring ceilings and low-slung black leather furniture. There's a huge ficus tree next to the desk. It's strung with white twinkle lights, probably a remnant of the long-past holiday season. It's oddly whimsical in the clean, minimalist setting.

I don't have time to admire the decor, though, because I'm too busy gaping at the twenty-foot-tall, floor-to-ceiling monitor. I've never seen a screen so big. Movie theater big.

A strand of DNA is displayed on the monitor. This is not just some run-of-the-mill textbook image. And it's definitely nothing like the primitive double helix model I made in sixth grade out of Styrofoam balls and toothpicks. (My mother's assessment: "What are we, Amish?")

This thing . . . this thing is pulsating with energy. It's alive.

"That's the project," my mother says. "That's 88715."

"It's real," I murmur.

"No, just a simulation. You can see the DNA, you can see entire chromosomes, you can pull out further—" She demonstrates by tracing a finger across the touch screen that is set at wheelchair level. The image on the wall zooms out. "Now you see a chromosome. Out further, it's a cell."

Solo locks my chair wheel and grabs a chair. He yawns. Clearly, he's not as mesmerized as I am.

"The best part is that you can use any number of different interfaces." Tap, tap, drag. "This one's made of Lego blocks, for younger kids. See how there's a Lego representation of the DNA?"

My mother's in the zone, her voice animated. She gets like this when she's excited about an idea. And this little project—this "fluff"—is nothing compared to her real work, the work she's overseen on new drug therapies. When she's laboring on something she's excited about, she'll move into Spiker's lab for days, even weeks, at a time. More than once, she's come home with her mascara smudged, her nails bitten to the quick, her eyes bleary.

Usually, it's because her team has failed. But sometimes, and there are just enough of those times, it's because they've succeeded.

"You can add or subtract blocks," my mother continues. "Hover over and you see what each does. Or"—tap, drag, tap—"you can picture each element as a colored blob or as a tile in a mosaic. But either way you can run forward and see the effect."

"The effect on what?"

"On your person."

"My what?"

"Your person." She enunciates carefully. "Per. Son. The person you're creating."

I lean forward and The Leg shifts slightly. "You almost sound like you're talking about a real human being."

She blinks and brushes back an errant strand of hair. "Don't be ridiculous. Of course it's not real. That would be illegal. The fines would be astronomical. The government would probably shut us down. I might even go to jail. Me!"

"I didn't—"

"No, no, no. This just provides students with an opportunity to learn how to . . ."

"To play God?" I supply.

She snaps her fingers. "Exactly. Exactly, exactly." Deep sigh. "Exactly. We want to enable the average person, a person like . . . like him"—her eyes flit toward Solo—"to understand what makes humans . . . human." She waves a dismissive hand and trails Bulgari.

"'Like him'?" I repeat.

"You know what I mean: Someone who's not a scientist."

"A mere mortal," Solo suggests.

"Stupidity is relative," my mother says, still addressing me. "And it's also case-specific. Thomas, the scientist most directly responsible for this project, has an IQ of 169. He also has his entire body covered in ridiculous tattoos. He's very smart at science. You, Eve, are very smart at school, particularly science, and very stupid at choosing your friends."

"Oh, snap," I say.

"What?"

"Sorry. I was flashing back to 2005."

The corners of Solo's mouth flirt with a smile.

"The point is, you get to play God."

"Can I play Portal instead?"

"You play Portal?" Solo asks.

"I have," I say cautiously. "Is it all right with you if a girl plays Portal?"

"A girl?" He's puzzled.

"Yes. I am, in fact, a girl."

"I noticed," he says.

"No, you did not notice she's a girl," my mother snarls. "You noticed she's my daughter."

My mother favors Solo with a look that has reduced many a grown man and woman to sniveling terror. She is in full feral mode.

But Solo is not afraid.

Oh, he pretends to be intimidated, but it's an act. I see it as plain as day. He's not intimidated at all. In fact, within his play-acting there's something deeper going on.

"Yes, ma'am," he says.

Oh my God. He hates her.

This startles me. I can't quite believe what I'm seeing in those eyes. He actually hates her.

I mean, I hate my mother, too, sometimes. But I'm her daughter. I'm supposed to.

And there are moments, like right now, when I actually kind of love her. At least, I love the way she loves her work.

Whatever's going on inside Solo's head, he hides it quickly. He slides his gaze to the side, away from her, and when he looks up his eyes are as distant and unknowable as a starless sky.

He has really nice lashes. Better than mine.

I look for something to do. I reach my hand toward the touch screen. Objects on the wall screen move.

"So I make a human," I say. "Is this just about how they look?"

"No, no, that would be a paint-by-numbers set." My mother smiles, but not at me. She's smiling at the computer-generated image. "No, if you're playing God, a lot of the fun is in building the brain. The mind."

She takes a step away. Her hands come up to form a sort of basket of fingers. It's one of her gestures. She uses it when lecturing her underlings.

"We are at a turning point in the evolution of the human species," she says, surveying, with slightly crazy eyes, an imaginary audience. "Evolution has blindly felt its way forward. Now we, the product of evolution, are taking the reins. We are taking the wheel."

"Is it the reins or the wheel?" I ask perkily, but she hears nothing.

"We will soon have the ability to design and create the new human. Evolution still, but guided evolution."

There is a long pause. I am not entirely sure if she expects us to applaud.

"Of course," she adds, coming down off her high, "only in computer simulation."

I don't know where she was headed with her lecture. But I am definitely sure that this project sounds interesting. The touch screen calls to me. Suddenly I'm wishing everyone would go away and let me play.

"I think I'll . . . you know. Just mess around with the program a little," I say.

My mother is pleased. Solo is . . . well, I can't exactly tell.

Ten minutes pass. I look up and I'm alone.

I didn't even notice them leave.

• • •

I STARE AT MY FIRST CHOICE. THE CHOICE I HAVE TO MAKE BEFORE I get into the details of playing God: male or female?

I consider the looming monitor.

Here's the thing: I am not beautiful.

I'm pretty. I'll allow that much. Pretty.

But I'm not the girl boys long for.

Cheerleader? No. Prom queen? No. Voted most likely to get a modeling contract? No.

It's not like I've spent my life beating the boys back with a flaming torch.

So. Am I "creating" a male or a female?

Worse yet . . . no, maybe it's *better* yet . . . I'm picky. Not so much about looks, although even there I'm kind of picky. It's more that I can't pretend some guy is interesting when he's not. If he's immature, I'll probably tell him so. Within five minutes of knowing him. And if he looks ridiculous dressed up like some wannabe, I'll probably say that, too, or more likely just steer clear of him.

When you're at a high school, looking around at the boys, and you subtract all the ones who are looking for Ms. Perfect, and subtract all the childish, ludicrous, boring, mean, or sex-obsessed ones, there aren't that many left.

It's not that I think I'm some kind of prize.

No, wait, that's not true. I do think I'm some kind of prize. I'm smart and occasionally funny and I'm pretty. I don't see why I should spend long dates with some guy who expresses himself in single syllables and wants to go to slasher movies.

Which does not answer the question: male or female?

I also don't understand why I should let some guy fondle me when I know the relationship has no future. I don't need to be groped that badly.

So I've been on exactly three dates. The first when I was fourteen. The most recent two years ago.

A guy tried to kiss me once. I didn't let him.

I live that part of my life vicariously through Aislin.

I hear her stories. And I admit I'm fascinated most of the time. Sometimes kind of appalled. And then fascinated again.

Sometimes I wonder what it would be like to be her. To be that . . . experimental. To be that "what the hell?". To actually have detailed, well-informed opinions on questions having to do with kissing. Or whatever.

I have no opinion on chest hair versus no chest hair. Aislin could write a treatise on that alone.

So. Who do I want to create with my new simulated godlike powers?

Male or female?

I sigh. I squirm in my wheelchair.

Who am I kidding?

Male.

— 11 —

SOLO

I can't get into Eve's file on Project 88715 yet. It's encrypted.

She just finished up a half hour ago, but I've already checked out the surveillance video. I can watch her face as she stares intently at the screen. I can even see myself, staring intently at . . . her. And Terra, being her predictably insane self, raving on about world domination.

I've been able to access—and edit—this kind of file for a couple of years now. I don't edit out the merely embarrassing, I make the minimal edits to conceal the degree to which I have penetrated security.

It bugs me that I can't get into Eve's working file. It's that new security protocol. A lot of the newer stuff is beyond my reach. But I have enough to bring the Food and Drug Administration down like a hurricane on this place.

Soon I may have enough to bring the FBI.

Do I want Terra Spiker to go to prison? The question makes me a little uncomfortable. She has sure as hell broken the law. Many laws.

It's time for school. It's Saturday, but I slacked off all week and I need to catch up. It won't take long; it never does. I click on the window for the online high school. I replaced the generic logo of the school with a picture of a guy sleeping. Which I guess says what I feel about it.

On my screen I get a video feed of a lecture on the Manhattan Project. Ancient history about the first atomic bomb.

The reading for this unit is on the right side of the screen in a window. There are numerous links in the text that open audio or video or text.

The lecturer drones into my headphones. I click on a link that shows a loop of an atomic bomb exploding.

A request for chat pops up. It's a kid I know online. He, she, or it goes by the name FerryRat7734.

FerryRat7734: What's vertical?
SnakePlissken: You could just say, "What's up?"

I don't know if FerryRat actually meant to write FurryRat. I don't ask questions of people I meet online. I figure they have a right to be whoever or whatever they want to be.

My online name is SnakePlissken. There's a reason for that.

It's the only character I've ever come across who shares my last name. Plissken. Google just the word "Plissken" and that's who you come up with. I don't appear in Google. I am invisible. That's deliberate.

> **FerryRat7734:** Is it just me or are they teaching us how to make an atomic bomb?
>
> **SnakePlissken:** The science is easy enough. The engineering's a bitch.
>
> **FerryRat7734:** So can you do me a favor? Send me your notes on the next week's lectures?
>
> **SnakePlissken:** You going on vacay?
>
> **FerryRat7734:** I wish. I have a procedure.

I sit back. The teacher is droning on. A second dialog box opens up with someone saying "How do you spell Openhimer?" I should answer that question, not ask FerryRat one of my own. I can sense I'm opening a can of worms. But how do you not follow up on something like that?

> **SnakePlissken:** What procedure?
>
> **FerryRat7734:** You don't want to know. Trust me.

I say that's not true, although it is. And I repeat the question. Lung transplant. FerryRat has cystic fibrosis, a genetic disease. Lung transplant is the final, desperation move.

SnakePlissken: Damn.

FerryRat7734: Exactly. So take notes, okay? I'm not
  dead yet.

SnakePlissken: Will do.

What else am I going to say? Someone tells you they're dying, what do you say? You say yes, I'll take notes.

It dawns on me for the first time that a lot of these online students that I know only by their handles, only from pop-up chat boxes, may be sick in one way or another.

It embarrasses me that I've never even considered this before.

"Slightly self-absorbed are you, Solo?" I mutter.

I sit through the rest of the lecture and then the natural history lesson after that.

Then I have work. Today I'm helping to prep visitors' suites for a conference. We have those about once a month. A bunch of Big Brains and Even Bigger Bucks fly in and we wine and dine and lecture them about the wonders of biotech and what a great investment Spiker is.

I'm distributing cut flowers to the rooms, checking the minibars, that kind of thing. Then I've got to fill in for the coffee cart guy for a few hours while he attends a wedding in Monterey.

I don't have to do this kind of work. Terra would let me stay here, keep a low profile, whatever. But the grunt work gives me access, and access is what I'm after.

When I'm done, I get into the system, mask my identity, and

start looking around for cystic fibrosis. Because as full of crap as Terra might be, and as much of a criminal as she might be, Spiker does do some amazing work.

There are lots of hits for CF. The company has done some research on it. But all files have been moved. They've all been transferred to Project 88715.

I Google "genetic diseases" and get a list.

Back to the Spiker database. I search for hemophilia. Many files. It seems we may be close to a gene-based cure. Transferred to Project 88715.

Neurofibromatosis. Ditto.

Sickle cell disease. Ditto.

Tay-Sachs disease. Ditto.

Not every genetic disease, but a lot. Too many for it to be some kind of fluke. Half a dozen major genetic diseases that Spiker has worked on have been suddenly transferred to Project 88715.

Why transfer all this info about genetic diseases to some ridiculous classroom software project?

I know the budget for all of Project 88715 is twelve million dollars. That's a lot of money, but it's not a lot of money at Spiker. At Spiker, anything under a billion is loose change.

I pull up the log entries—the brief descriptions—for CF and hemophilia and the rest. Rough addition in my head: The total budget is over twenty-eight billion dollars.

Billion. With a "B."

Twenty-eight *billion* dollars' worth is suddenly under the aegis of a twelve-*million*-dollar project?

That's like saying your local grocery store chain will be managed by the kids selling lemonade on the street corner.

Terra Spiker's up to something. I don't know exactly what yet.

But I will find out.

EVƎ

"Mmmmm. Caviar," Aislin says.

It's one of her phrases.

It's late afternoon, and Solo has just entered my room. He's holding Aislin's shoulder bag.

Aislin has no self-editing function. She is incapable of ever not saying what she's thinking.

"I'm sorry?" Solo says.

"It's expensive. It's . . . delicious. And I could eat it with a spoon." She's employing her purring, hair-tossing, flank-stroking voice, one that brings an alarmed expression to Solo's face. He's probably not used to girls like Aislin.

Come to think of it, almost no one is used to girls like Aislin because there's only one Aislin.

God, I've missed her.

"Leave him alone, Aislin," I say mildly.

What can I say? I like the girl. She's the polar opposite of me.

"Oh, is he yours, E.V.?" Aislin asks innocently. She's about six inches away from Solo. "Can I at least have . . . the leftovers?"

Aislin is tall, taller than I am, and I'm not short. She's wearing shorts which, if they were any shorter, would qualify as the bottom of a bathing suit, and she has about a mile of leg. Her T-shirt might as well be spray paint. She has sleek, short, stylish copper hair and eyes that slant up, giving her an exotic, feline look.

And breasts. Which she deploys with absolutely cynical yet devastating effect.

I love myself and my body and I'm proud of being who I am blah blah blah. But there are times when I would give a lot to have Aislin's body and her boldness.

She knows no fear, Aislin.

No, that's not true. She *shows* no fear.

"Your bag," Solo says, leaning back with his eyes wide and voice a little trembly. "It's uh . . . security . . . you know." He shoots a panicky look at me.

I shrug. I'm not rescuing you, dude. I look down to conceal an anticipatory grin because I know what's coming.

Aislin takes the bag from Solo, but before he can escape, she clamps a hand on his wrist. She opens the bag and examines its contents. "So I guess they took my flask."

"They said something about your personal property being returned when you leave."

Good boy, Solo: a complete sentence.

"Wait!" Aislin says. She reaches into the bag and then, yes, draws out a long string of condoms. "At least," she says, "they didn't take anything I really . . . need."

A strange whinnying sound comes from Solo. He flees the room.

Aislin laughs, delighted. She perches on the edge of my bed and I say, "You are such a bitch."

"I know, aren't I?"

"You have no idea how much I've missed you." I sigh. "I miss everything. I miss homework. I miss the very special stench that is the girls' locker room."

"Nerd. School's over in a few days, anyway. They'll let you make it all up in the fall." Aislin pats The Leg. "Oh, crap, sorry! Did I hurt you?"

"No, actually. The pain pills work really well."

"Don't suppose you have any extra you feel like sharing?"

I breathe in deeply. "How's Maddox?"

"Who?" she asks. "I'm sorry, that name slipped right out of my brain when I saw Mr. Scruffy McMuscles."

"His name is Solo."

She grins a huge, lascivious grin. "Why, of course it is. But he could be in a duo without too much trouble." She switches on her serious face. "Maddox is out on bail. If he doesn't screw up again they'll probably let him go with community service."

"If," I say.

I know it's wrong, but Aislin's troubles are almost reassuring to me, they're such a regular feature of our lives.

I first met Aislin in sixth grade. My dad had died over the summer, and she provided much-needed distraction. Even then, she was the glamorous fashionista, and at a point where I was still four years away from noticing that boys existed as something different and apart and interesting, Aislin was already charming them like a cobra mesmerizing prey.

She was also the only one who could make me laugh that horrible year.

"You know Maddox," Aislin said. She looks down and away, her patented move to ensure I don't know how much something is bothering her.

When he goes off to prison—and he will, someday—Aislin will probably wait for him. Her loyalty is fierce.

I love her.

"So what are you doing in here for fun?" she asks.

"Help me get into my wheelchair and I'll show you," I say.

It takes a while, but we manage to haul my giant leg and bruised body into my wheelchair.

Except, now that I think about it, *am* I bruised anymore?

"Push me over to the mirror," I say.

It's a floor-to-ceiling mirror, gilt-framed.

I brace for the worst. I saw myself early on, a reflection in a piece of shiny equipment: It was not good. I had huge raccoon eyes, my nose was red, and there were two visible bumps on my forehead, one of which was about the size of an egg yolk.

Since then, I've been avoiding mirrors.

I stare at my reflected image in disbelief.

I'm me.

"Huh," I say. Where are my bruises? My egg yolk? "Push me closer."

"It's kind of hard to believe you almost died," Aislin says. "It's only been, like, a few days."

"It's nuts," I say. "I mean, my eyes were all . . ." I wave my hand around my face. "I looked like I'd been hit by a train. With good reason. I shouldn't be this . . ."

Aislin shrugs. "Yeah, but this isn't a regular hospital, right?"

"No, you're right, it isn't," I say. "My mother was completely freaked about getting me out of San Fran and into this place. I guess she was onto something."

While I contemplate my reflection, Aislin pokes around the room. "Giant flat-screen, nice sound system. Maybe I should get run over."

"I had stitches here," I murmur, peeling back a strip of surgical tape. "Right here on my cheek. Now there's nothing."

"Lucky," Aislin says. "Would've been hard to cover with makeup." She slides open my closet doors. "Whoa. Primo robes. Can I steal one?"

I glance at the closet. My sketchbook is on the top shelf, barely visible. "Hey, can you get that down for me? My mother probably had someone stash it there."

"Have I mentioned that your mother's an ice-cold bitch?"

"I believe you may have mentioned that in passing, yes." I hold up my cell phone. "At least she finally let me have my phone back. Charged and everything."

Aislin stands on tiptoe and retrieves the sketchbook. She browses through the pages, holds one up for me to see.

"I love this guy. You've been working on him forever."

"He's a cartoon. He has no depth. No soul."

"Screw depth."

"I can't get the eyes right."

"Hmm. Maybe. But he's got great lips." She taps her chin with her index finger. "You know, he reminds me a little of what's-his-name. So-hot."

"Solo."

"Needs a body, though. Your drawing, I mean. So-hot's doing just fine in that department." She smirks. "If you need suggestions, I can help you finish him. If you know what I mean."

I ignore her. "Must be genetic. My dad never could do faces, either."

"But he was a sculptor."

"Sculpting, drawing. Same problems." I stare out the window at the undulating hills wreathed in fog. "I remember once he tried to draw my mother. He was using oil pastels, I think. He gave up after a couple tries."

"Must've been tough, capturing Satan on canvas." Aislin places the sketchbook on my bedside table. "Hey, can you draw, anyway? With your arm all mummied up like that?"

"Nah." I consider my crushed hand. "Although the way things are going, who knows?"

"So where's the minibar?"

"There's a fridge in that cabinet with sodas in it."

Aislin pulls a flask from the back waistband of her shorts. Naturally, security only found the one in her purse: who carries more than one?

She takes a swig and holds the flask out to me. "Cough syrup?"

"You mean vodka?" I ask. I don't want to show disapproval, I really don't, because it bothers her when I do and it creates a barrier between us.

"Lemon vodka, cough syrup, who can tell the difference, really?" Aislin asks.

"I'm actually tempted," I say. "But, no."

"You're on meds."

"Plus I don't really drink."

"You've had beer."

"Don't get caught or my mother will ban you. And listen to me, Aislin: I'm all alone in here. I need you."

She acts tough. But she gets tears in her eyes and gives me a hug. "Don't worry, no one will keep me away from you," she says. "Now, let's go find Mr. Bashful. I'll tell him you like him."

"I will kill you if you say any such thing!"

"Yeah, right: You're in a wheelchair. You're not that scary."

"There's something else I want to show you first."

Aislin steers me toward the door. "What is it?"

"I'm making my own male."

She frowns. "Mail, like e-mail?"

"Male, like m-a-l-e."

"You have my full attention, girl."

– 13 –

SOLO

So. She has a friend. Not at all the kind of friend I would have expected.

Interesting.

I watch from the end of the hallway as Eve and Aislin head toward the elevator. Aislin's pushing the wheelchair at full throttle. Eve is cracking up.

Man, she has a great laugh.

How to do this without being obvious? She's not dumb, Eve, she'll know I'm trying to get to know her if I just keep accidentally running into her.

I *do* need to know her, at least a little. Not as a girl, of course—although she is definitely, well, that. But that's not really the point.

You're so full of it, Solo. Of course that's part of it. Why not be honest with yourself and admit that's part of it?

Yes, okay, yes, you need to get to know her in order to decide whether she's useful. But dude. Solo. Dude: That's not all of it.

I decide to let it go. Let Eve and her friend have some time. I don't need to push it right now. Plus I have work to do.

I watch them rolling away.

Damn.

I don't like them being here. I've gotten along so far in life without so-called peers. I have some people I talk to online. Actual humans my own age, really not important.

And yet I almost can't resist the magnetic pull as they head into the elevator.

The elevator doors slide shut. "Damn," I say, resisting my desire to punch something.

My phone buzzes with a text. It's work, of course. It's not like my twenty closest friends have my number. It'll be someone needing a doughnut, or a rack of instruments run through the autoclave, or some forgotten thing fetched from a car in the parking lot. In theory it could be one of my online teachers, but that's unlikely: I keep up with my work. It's not a strain.

I check my screen. Tattooed Tommy wants a cappuccino and a poppy-seed bagel.

I groan, head to the elevator. I push "7" and I'm whisked to The Meld, the incredible space where the Big Brains hang out. It's a vast open area—you could park a passenger jet in it—but it's broken up into pods of moveable workstations. It's like they took the cubicles from every boring office on earth—one wall, plus a desk and chair and all of that—and rigged them so they could be driven around.

Each workstation has an electric motor and four nylon wheels. They form into groups and they break apart and re-form into different groups. You never know where any of the individual Big Brains might be just by looking, but we have an app that shows current locations. I know, for example, that Tattooed Tommy, the crazy-smart biochemist from Berkeley, is at grid J-7.

In the kitchen, I grab the coffee cart. Caffeine in various forms, organic herbal tea, bagels, muffins, energy bars. This isn't my job, but I don't mind covering for the regular dude. There's no better way to find out what's going on than by being a peon everyone ignores. If you're the coffee guy, it's just assumed that you don't understand anything you see on the computer screens, holographic displays, and even the occasional old-school chalkboard.

In a place filled with people who think of themselves as Big Brains, a guy dishing out fruit cups is invisible. No one notices when I seem to be checking e-mail on my phone, but I'm actually taking a picture or hitting the "record" voice memo button. I've got a pretty good memory, and that helps, too.

I pause and take a swig from my water bottle. Karen, one of the biochem research assistants, grabs a cheese Danish off my cart. "You get a promotion?" she asks.

I shrug, move on, keep my eyes open. It's hard to steal data here, very hard. But not impossible.

My biggest problem: At Spiker Biopharm, we don't do cloud.

It's a security thing. Everyone uploads data to the cloud. That's where people have their pictures, their tunes, their manuscripts, whatever. But Spiker isn't "whatever," so all Spiker data goes strictly to in-house servers.

No CD burners. No USB ports for thumb drives.

Which makes it very complicated for me to steal data. And yet . . .

There's a file in the cloud. I've encrypted it so heavily the CIA couldn't break in. People usually use a four- or five-character security code. My code is thirty-two characters long.

I comfort myself with this knowledge as I make my way toward Tommy.

"Bagel and a capp, right?" I ask.

He's around thirty. Covered in tattoos, everywhere except his hands, neck, and his face. Even his forehead has the word "Pixies"—that's an alt-rock band—in gothic script.

Tommy thinks of himself as a cool guy. He's nice to me, in the condescending way that a person who's always been the smartest guy in the room is nice to someone he sees as inferior.

"Poppy seed?" he asks.

"Poppy seed," I confirm.

He takes the food, sighs, and shakes his head. "Hey, kid. Have you met the girl?"

I guess what girl he means, but I need to play dumb. "What girl?"

"The kid. The daughter. I don't know her name."

"You mean Evening Spiker? Yeah, I met her."

He looks at me doubtfully. He's judging whether I can answer his next question. He's wondering whether even communicating with me is a waste of time.

"What's the deal with her? She bright? Stupid? What?"

I shrug. Because I'm just a peasant and that's what dumb teenagers do. "She seems pretty smart, I guess. Why?"

He shakes his head, irritated. The questions are only supposed to go in one direction. But he's Tattooed Tommy, so he has to maintain his reputation for not being an a-hole. "Boss is tasking her. On something of mine. Amateur hour." His eyes flicker, he's said too much, he's come too close to criticizing Terror Spiker.

I shrug again. "She can't be doing much. She's pretty messed up."

"Yeah, maybe," Tommy says confidently, "but I'm guessing she'll recover amazingly well."

"I hope so," I say. And I think, yeah, she *will* recover amazingly. And thanks for confirming you know that, poppy-seed man.

"Anyway, it's nothing," Tommy adds. "The software she's playing with. Just some widget I threw together one night when I was seriously stoned."

"Terror was showing it to her this morning," I say. "Project 88 something?"

"Yeah." Tommy sips his cappuccino. "Yeah, like I say, it's crap. A brain fart."

"Another bagel?" I ask.

"Nah."

"Later, then." I wheel away.

A brain fart.

Whatever you say, Tommy.

I know a thing or two about Project 88715, and it's a whole lot more than some educational widget you threw together after a couple bong hits.

It's more than a glittering strand of DNA on a giant monitor.

More than a toy that Terra's using to keep Eve occupied.

This much I know already: When Tommy and the Big Brains, in whispered, wry asides, talk about Project 88715, they call it something else.

They call it the "Adam Project."

14

EVƎ

"So when do we get to make his unit?" Aislin asks, staring up at the giant monitor.

"His what?"

"Exactly. His 'what.' His 'Whoa, what is that?' His area."

"Are you referring to his boy parts?" I am trying to sound indifferent. Indifferent doesn't really work well with the phrase "boy parts." But in my embarrassment I can't come up with a better phrase.

"Did you just actually say 'boy parts'?" Aislin asks, rolling a chair over.

"You have to do things in order. That's how the software works," I explain. "First it has you decide about the simple physical things. This morning I worked on the eyes."

"You mean *his* eyes." Aislin watches me tap away at my keyboard. "You are making a male, right?"

I nod.

"Atta girl."

Tap, tap, click. I really love this software. It's like making art, without the gut-wrenching fear of failure. Creation, with a handy-dandy "delete" key.

I tap something called a "Show Me" button. The screen on the wall shows two enormous irises. Just irises. No whites, nothing else.

"Yuck!" Aislin exclaims. "What the hell are those?"

"Irises. I gave him hazel eyes."

"How come?"

"I don't know. I've never really known anyone with eyes that color. Maybe that's why."

It's fascinating, the way they've designed this software. There are a bunch of genes that deal with the simple matter of eye color. You drop them into a sort of grid. The grid—which in this version has been designed to look like a very long string of beads—has a lot of the "beads" already filled in. That leaves plenty of blank spots for me to pick and choose.

I can increase or decrease the magnification. At life-size they're invisibly small. Blown up, they're six feet in diameter. Zoom in all the way and you get into the nano scale, where they don't have color at all. They're just bumpy gray cells.

Aislin puts her boots up on the desk and leans back, hands laced behind her head. "This is creeping me out. Do something un-gross."

I add very white whites to the eyes. "Okay, now the capillaries," I say, scanning my choice menu.

"Let's do abs instead."

"I told you: It won't let me. Besides, this is the fun part. All the details."

"Uh-huh." Aislin is unconvinced.

I choose small capillaries and Aislin nods her approval. "Don't want him getting bloodshot too easily."

I stare at my creation. "I'm not sure about the iris color. It's kind of muddy."

"What's your fantasy eye color?"

"I don't have one," I say, because I'm pretty sure I don't.

Aislin scowls.

I change the irises to blue.

"More," Aislin says.

Tap, tap. They're an intense, mountain-lake-at-twilight blue. "Bingo."

"Next up," I say, "visual acuity. Should I make him just a little near-sighted?"

"No," Aislin says firmly. "No glasses. No contacts, even."

I pause to consider. Everyone should have flaws. Isn't that what makes us interesting? Isn't that what keeps us from just being carbon copies of each other?

A slight adjustment in the shape of the eye and the lens, and he's wearing Coke-bottle lenses the rest of his simulated life.

"Okay, you win." I opt for perfect vision. I can always change my mind later.

"How old are these eyes, anyway?" Aislin asks.

"Part of the fun of the simulator is that I can choose the age of my person. I can make him a baby. Or I can age him all the way up until he's as old as one of those sparkly vampires." I grin. "But that would be creepy."

Somehow making a baby seems way too close to reality. Who wants a baby? Later, okay, in ten years, or twenty. Or thirty. Not now. The safe answer—at least this is what I tell myself—is to make him about my age.

"Um, I don't know how old he should be. Maybe seventeen?"

"Eighteen," Aislin says firmly.

"Eighteen, then."

Tap, tap. The color of the irises comes into sharper focus. The whites are just a little less translucent.

The system prompts me: *Blood supply needed to achieve viability.*

Yes, of course blood supply, but does it have to be right this minute?

"The computer's blinking at you," Aislin says, pointing at the screen.

"The eyes need blood."

"Ick."

"I can do a whole heart and circulatory system," I say, reading my options. "Or I can attach a temporary artificial blood supply."

"Do the second one." Aislin cocks her head at the giant monitor. "It's easier."

The picture on the wall shifts. It's hard to spot at first. But even the best special effects have a slight air of unreality about them. The images I've been seeing are amazing, but now merely amazing is becoming spectacular.

I could swear those two eyes, white balloons trailing unconnected nerve endings, I could swear they're real. They look exactly as if they're suspended in clear liquid. The veins and arteries going to and from the eye are attached to a plastic tube that pulsates gently at the rhythm of a human heart.

"Disgusting," Aislin pronounces.

"But cool," I say.

Aislin's phone beeps and she checks the message. "Maddox," she says, in a tone that's both elated and apologetic. It's the special voice she reserves for dumping me. "Sorry, I gotta go."

"No!" I cry, grabbing her arm with my good hand. "You just got here!"

"He's freaked about something or other." Aislin stands and stretches. "You know how he gets."

Yes. I do know. And I really can't stand the guy sometimes. But I know enough not to say what I'm thinking.

"Look, it's the weekend. I can come by tomorrow and play."

"Okay," I pout. "But if I get to the good stuff on my guy, I'm doing it without you." I sigh. I don't want to be lonely again. "You want the limo to drive you back to town?"

"Nah. Maddox is picking me up. I'm good." Aislin leans down and hugs me. "I love you, you know."

"Me, too."

"Want a push back to your room?"

I gaze at the huge blue eyes hovering before me like twin earths. "I think I'll stay awhile. I'm kind of getting into this."

Aislin pauses at the door. "Know what?"

"What?"

"I'm really glad you're okay." She waves at the floating eyes. "Bye, Mr. Eyeballs."

Aislin's almost out the door when she pauses. "He needs a name, E.V." She purses her lips. "Well, duh," she says, snapping her fingers. "Bye, Adam," she calls, and then she's gone.

Adam. I guess if you're going to create a man, you pretty much have to call him Adam.

I don't really like the name, though. All my life I've insisted that people call me "Evening" or "E.V.," anything but "Eve." Eve leads inevitably to Adam and Eve, and that leads to forbidden fruit and the whole nudity thing. When you're in middle school that entire conversation tends to go off the rails.

I wonder if Adam here, Mr. Eyeballs, would object to being called Adam on those same grounds. It feels hypocritical of me to acquiesce to "Adam" just because my unimaginative mother came up with "Eve."

I could call him Ad for short. Or Dam.

Or Steve, for that matter.

"What do you—"

"Ahhh!" I jump about an inch out of my wheelchair. I brace for the wave of pain that should come from such a sudden movement, but my leg does not cry out in protest.

Thank God for the pain meds.

It's Solo, pushing some kind of cart. How long has he been standing behind me?

"Hey," I mutter. "Don't you knock?"

"No door," he points out accurately.

"Well, give me some sign that you're sneaking up on me! Clear your throat or something!"

"Ahem," he says, clearing his throat. He pushes the cart close to me. "Eyes, huh?" he asks, looking past me at the disembodied eyeballs.

"Yes." I want to follow up with something sarcastic, but I draw a blank because I've turned to look at him and I notice now, how could I not notice, that the eyes I've created from scratch are Solo's eyes.

"What's that color called?" he asks.

"Just . . . I . . . I'm changing it. I was trying for blue."

"You like blue eyes, huh?"

"Yes. I do. I like blue eyes."

"I thought you might want something to eat." He takes a paper sack off the cart.

"Kind of late for lunch, isn't it?" The clock in the corner of the display reads 03:17 P.M. "How do you know I didn't already eat lunch?" I ask, just as my stomach growls loudly.

"Intuition," he says with a straight face.

I save my work on Adam and log out.

"Come on, we don't want to eat in here," Solo says. Without waiting for my approval, he plops the bag of food on my lap and takes the grips of my wheelchair.

"What about your cart?"

He shrugs. "What about it?"

We go down a level, through a hallway, across yet another open space full of grown-up toys for the Big Brains, and out onto a vast deck overlooking the bay. It's not the million-dollar view you might get in Tiburon, which faces the city, but it's not bad. The fog has lifted, and we have a good view of the Richmond–San Rafael Bridge. There's a tanker riding low, slowly cutting through the water like a migrating whale. If I could somehow look around the corner past Angel Island, I'd be able to see the city. And it bugs me that I can't. I miss my home, my school, my city.

There's a group of four, kind of glum, munching at a table twenty yards away, too far for us to overhear them. We spread the food out on a picnic table. Sandwiches, chips, two puddings, one chocolate, one vanilla.

"From the cafeteria?" I ask, pulling one of the sandwiches apart to find turkey and Brie.

"They're good," Solo says. "Say one thing for your mom: She takes care of her employees."

"Yes, I noticed. You know what they don't have? Double-double, animal style."

He nods. "You're an In-N-Out fan?"

"Mostly I want it because I can't get it," I admit. "I also want some Coldstone. And I'm having a weird craving for the awful Beef-a-roni they serve on alternate Thursdays at my school. Also . . . Never mind."

"No, go on. I find it interesting. Knowing what you miss about normal life."

I take a bite of sandwich and wash it down with a swig of sparkling water with lime.

"Okay. I miss Zachary's. Best pizza in SF. I miss having to get ready for school, waiting at the bus stop—"

"You don't have a limo?"

I make a face. "She's offered. My mother, I mean."

"But you don't want to show up at school in a limo."

"It kind of marks you as a douche."

"Yep."

"There are kids at my school who get dropped off in limos."

"Private school?"

I laugh. "I tried once to get her to send me to a public school. I thought I'd like to meet some kids who don't have maids but whose moms are maids."

"Poor little rich girl," Solo says.

Maybe I should take offense. But the cool breeze kind of drains the nasty from me. "I miss regular life. Or my version of it, anyway. School."

"But you can't leave because of your leg."

What an interesting way he has of saying it. It's not a question. It's not quite a statement. It's almost a challenge.

"How much does it hurt?" Solo asks.

"It . . . it doesn't," I say. "But that's because of the pain meds, of course."

He looks down at his food and chews. He has something to say, but he's considering it. "Have you seen it without the bandages? I mean, have you seen the actual leg?"

I shake my head. "Not . . . no." I frown at him, and he studies the placid water. How does he know I haven't seen the wound? "I asked. They said it was still too bad. They didn't want to upset me."

A knowing smirk comes and goes. "Yeah."

I push the sandwich aside. "Who the hell are you?" I demand.

"Solo Plissken."

"I didn't ask your name," I say. "Who *are* you? Why are you here? You're not old enough to be doing a full-time job at a place like Spiker."

"Does it always take you this long to start asking obvious questions?"

My face burns. "I'm asking now."

"I'm your mother's ward. When my parents died six years ago she sort of, well, inherited me."

The math is simple. And yet I'm sitting here, astounded. "She's been your guardian for six years? And she's never mentioned it to me?"

He looks at me straight, eye to eye. "I wonder why that is?"

Suddenly I am very uncomfortable. He knows things I don't. He knows things he hasn't told me. Why the hell am I finding things out about my mother from this guy?

I take a breath, try to focus. "What happened to your parents?"

Again, that fleeting smirk. "The safe question. Or maybe you're going to sneak up on the truth, little by little."

"If you don't want to answer—"

"Car accident. No big story there. No mystery. I was at my grandmother's. They were on vacation. Without me." He pauses, takes a swig from his water bottle. "Good thing I wasn't with them. They went off the side of a road, down an embankment. Crash. Boom."

I flash back to my dad's death. The insistent knocking on the door, the grim-faced cops, my mother's agonized scream.

Imagine losing both your parents in the blink of an eye.

"I'm sorry," I say quietly. "That must have been horrible for you." I tear a strip from my napkin. "My dad . . . well, he died when I was young, too. Why didn't you go live with your grandmother?"

"She's eighty-seven. She thinks Roosevelt is president."

"Why my mother, though? Because she's so warm and nurturing?"

He laughs. And he has a nice laugh. Damn. I wish he didn't have such a nice laugh. He's a temporary blip in my life. He's not my type. Except for the laugh. Maybe the eyes. Not the smirk, or the hair which needs cutting so badly my fingers are itching to grab the knife and do it myself.

"Your mother and my parents were business partners."

"So . . . you own part of Spiker?"

Solo shakes his head. "No. My parents were screwed out of the business by your mother."

This does not entirely surprise me. Still, for some reason, I feel vaguely guilty. Sins of the mother and all that.

"I guess your dad—he was still alive then—tried to make peace. But it wasn't happening. Up until then they had all been best friends. My folks died before they could change the will that left me to your mother's tender mercies."

"You hate her," I say.

Solo doesn't react right away. He thinks. He cups his chin in his hand and carefully considers.

Finally he says, "I don't do hate." He grins ruefully. "However, I do resentment pretty well."

I want to ask Solo more, much more, but my phone chimes. A text.

Need u now. Bad.

When I dial Aislin, the call doesn't connect. I check my phone: one bar. Figures. Just enough for a text to get through.

"Damn," I murmur. Aislin in trouble? Not a surprise. Aislin texting me for help? That is unusual. Generally, she just stumbles through her escapades, then regales me with the details later.

"Aislin?" Solo inquires.

Another text. *Where r u? Guys after M at GGP. Going there 2 help.*

"Damn," I murmur. "Aislin's idiot boyfriend's in trouble. He's at Golden Gate Park, and she thinks she's going to save his butt."

"What kind of trouble?"

"You mean felony or misdemeanor?" I rub my eyes. "You never know with Maddox."

I text her back. *WAIT. I'll think of something.*

"I don't know what to do," I tell Solo. "I can't leave this place, not with . . . The Leg. Dr. Anderson told me not to put any pressure on it."

"Dr. Anderson is a tool."

I shift The Leg back and forth, a couple inches in each direction. No pain. Nothing.

Solo gives a small, approving nod.

I meet his eyes. "If I needed to, say, disappear from here for a couple of hours without being caught, could you help me do it?"

There's an intriguing arrogance in his face. "Talk to me."

15

I'M SEEING AN INTERESTING SIDE TO SOLO. HE'S NOT THE BLUSHING BOY IN MY hospital room, rendered speechless by Aislin's antics. He's totally in control, coolly pushing my wheelchair through maintenance areas and unused kitchen facilities and darkened labs.

As we move, he provides muted commentary. Things like, "This room hasn't been used probably ever, so I turned off surveillance cameras. . . . The camera on this part of the stairwell is broken. . . . I can delete tape of this later—no one will notice. . . . The scientist who works in this space is a paranoid so no camera. . . . Infrared is off here so as long as we don't turn on the light . . ."

What I'm coming to think of as "Escape from Spiker" involves about sixty different, distinct steps, all inside Solo's head. The building is massive, but he has it memorized—every door, room, and camera angle.

We reach a set of steps. "How do we get down those?" I ask.

"I carry you. Then I come back up and get your wheelchair."

"I don't think so."

"You want out or not?"

"You don't look that strong." I say it, but it's a lie. He does look that strong.

Another text from Aislin. *Maddox in trubble.*

Spelling is not Aislin's favorite thing.

"Lean forward," Solo says.

I do, and his hand goes behind my back. I feel his arms slide over the clasp of my bra.

"I'm going to lift The Leg."

"I'm afraid it will hurt."

"It won't," he says, and I wonder what makes him so sure. His palm slides under my thighs and with barely a grunt he has me up and out of my chair. My face is close to his, close enough that his hair brushes my cheek and my nose and I have to fight an urge to sneeze.

I ask myself what I ate at lunch. I ask myself why I didn't bother with deodorant this morning.

I ask myself whether that's the smell of his shampoo or just the smell of him. Either way, I like it. In fact, whatever it is, and I'm not saying I know, I find it strangely fascinating.

He carries me down the stairs, kneels, places me on the next-to-bottom step, and runs back up to grab my wheelchair.

I don't turn around to watch him climb away, because that would be me checking out his butt. Which is not something I would ever do.

But his jeans fit. No sagging for Solo.

I insist on climbing into my chair on my own. It's easier than it should be. We're back in gear, and a few minutes later, we arrive at an underground garage.

Solo touches my shoulder. "We have to be careful here," he warns.

We wait just inside a recessed doorway in a corner of the garishly lit concrete-plus-more-concrete space.

"Do you have a car?" I ask.

"I have a dozen cars," he replies. "Oddly enough, they're all identical."

He points to a sort of car corral where a dozen or so electric cars are parked. Each one has the Spiker logo on the side.

Solo checks the clock on his phone. He looks up and within a few seconds a guard comes walking by. We hear the footsteps. Coming, then going, fading altogether.

"Yep," Solo says. He pushes me out into the garage. The cars aren't locked. The "keys" rest on the dashboard.

Solo pushes the passenger seat back as far as it will go and I hoist myself in. He folds my chair and pops it into the trunk. The car starts without a sound.

"Do you know how to drive?" I ask.

"Do you have six dollars in cash?" Solo asks, ignoring my question.

"I don't exactly have my purse with me."

"Check the glove compartment. See if there's a roll of quarters."

I dig under some maps and find two rolls.

"Good. We have to use cash at the bridge."

I point to the automatic toll-road transponder mounted on the windshield.

"Yeah," he says. "Pull that down and put it in the glove compartment. We don't want to be tracked. I don't want to have to try to hack the toll system."

"But you have no problem hacking into Spiker?" I ask.

An annoyed look, maybe even an angry one, clouds Solo's eyes.

"Seat belt," he says tersely.

I click my belt and we're off across the garage with an almost silent whir of electric motors. The tires on the painted concrete floor make more noise.

"Lower the sun visor and put your head down," he orders. "Cameras."

There's an automated checkout. Solo pulls a plastic ID card from his pocket. I can see the picture is not of him. The name on the ID is Wanda Chang.

"Funny, you don't look Chinese," I say.

He swipes the card past the reader. The gate goes up.

And for the first time in forever, I am outside.

"They'll never know?" I ask, looking anxiously back at the receding outer gate of the campus.

He shrugs. "I can't guarantee that. They know I escape from time to time."

"Escape?" Even though I've been feeling the same way, it seems overly dramatic.

"What else is it when the monkey gets out of his cage?"

"You're not a monkey," I point out. "You're strange, but you're human."

"Mostly," he says with a slim smile.

"But you *can* leave, right?"

"Yeah. But where would I go, exactly? I don't have wheels"—he takes a sharp right—"not unless I get them this way. And Spiker's out in the middle of nowhere."

It's twenty minutes to the Golden Gate Bridge, which, as usual, is shrouded in fog. I call Aislin to tell her I'm on my way, but she doesn't answer.

When we reach Aislin's townhouse, I text her that I'm outside. She appears a moment later, running down the steps. She's upset. Her nose is red and mascara rings her eyes. But she still has time to do a double take when she sees Solo behind the wheel.

"Sorry I couldn't pick up when you called. I was talking to Maddox." Aislin slides into the backseat. She sighs dramatically, but the effect is ruined by the fact that she's really worried, not just playing at it.

"Thanks for coming." She manages a smile for Solo. "And you brought me a toy to play with on the way. How thoughtful."

"So what's wrong?" I ask.

"Maddox. Of course," she says. "He's trapped."

"Trapped where?"

"In the park."

"And he's trapped there *why*?" I ask.

"Some guys. They think he owes them money. He's in the park and they're after him."

"Can't he call the police?" Solo asks.

"That would be . . . embarrassing." Aislin digs through her purse and retrieves some lip gloss. She slides it on expertly, no mirror required. "They might decide to search him."

"Ah," Solo says. "He's carrying . . . ?"

"Some weed. He has to sell it to get the money he needs to pay off the dudes chasing him."

Solo stares at me, expressionless. I smile feebly. Shrug.

He's going to turn the car around and take us straight back to Spiker, and I don't blame him.

Solo pulls into traffic. "I can't believe your mom thinks Aislin's a bad influence," he says. "I think she's kind of fun."

16

THERE AREN'T A LOT OF ROADS INSIDE GOLDEN GATE PARK. THE PARK IS HUGE, bigger than Central Park in New York. It's a long rectangle with one end up against Haight Street—hippie town—and the other end right up against the Pacific Ocean. From weed to waves, you might say.

"Where is he in the park?" Solo asks as he takes a tight turn, narrowly missing an old woman on a wobbly bike.

"He's in a lake," Aislin says.

"Of course he is," I say under my breath.

"In a lake?" Solo repeats. "In the water?"

"On an island."

I pull out my phone. "I'll Google a map of the park." When the map glows on screen, I groan. "There are a lot of lakes. Like twenty or more."

Solo streaks through a yellow light. "Any with islands?" he asks.

We've reached the edge of the park. "Is it a big island or a small island?" I ask Aislin. "A lot of them have islands."

She fires off a text as Solo pulls onto John. F. Kennedy Drive, the road that runs the length of the north side of the park. Traffic is light. The sun is dropping from view and shadows are lengthening beneath the trees.

"He says how big is big?" Aislin reads from her phone.

"That's an excellent philosophical question," I say. "Ask him how long it would take for him to walk across it."

It takes several minutes of texting—Maddox is not, shall we say, academically gifted—before we decide he's on an island in something called Mallard Lake.

I set the GPS on the dashboard.

"Make a U-turn," a female voice instructs, in a tone that suggests we've already disappointed her.

Solo brakes. "I don't think it's legal to."

"Now make a U-turn," the voice commands.

Solo pulls the car into a tight U-turn.

"Turn right in a hundred yards," says the voice.

"What do we do when we get there?" I ask Aislin. "These guys, the guys after Maddox—"

"Now turn right."

"—they're not like people who would have guns, right?"

"Turn right in one-half mile."

"Guns?" Aislin echoes. Like she's never heard the word before. "They might, but—"

"Whoa," I say.

"—what are they going to do, shoot us?" She attempts a laugh. It fails.

Aislin reaches up from the backseat and switches on the radio. It's Rancid, singing about another East Bay night. One of my favorites, despite the fact that it's partly about earthquakes and watching the freeways fall. (Before my time, that quake.)

Even though I like the song, I reach to switch it off. Solo stops me, snatching my wrist in midair. He's as quick as a snake. "It's good cover. Makes us seem like regular kids."

He rolls down the windows. The air is damp and smells of pine.

"Now turn right," says the voice.

The lake is close by, but you can't see it from the road. We see it on the GPS map. It's an isosceles triangle with a circular island in the fat end. The park isn't busy and there are only a few cars parked here and there. But at the point where the road is closest to the lake, there are three cars, obviously hastily parked.

"That's Maddox's stepfather's brother's wife's Ford!" Aislin cries.

The Ford, a dented tan Fusion, is boxed in by the other two cars, a tricked-out Miata and a Civic with spinners and a spoiler.

The Miata's driver's-side door is open. No one is inside.

Solo slows down and pulls off onto the shoulder. We are surrounded by way too many trees and way too many bushes. It's surprisingly jungle-esque for something in the middle of San Francisco.

Our radio plays on after Solo turns off the engine. "Text your boyfriend that we're here," he instructs.

"He says he can't move," Aislin reports back.

Solo cranks the music higher. "Ask him if he hears the music."

Maddox hears the music.

"If he hears it so do . . . Okay, here they come," Solo says. There's a look of satisfaction on his face. "Seat belts tight?"

"Why?" I ask.

Two guys, both Asian, thin, smoking cigarettes, emerge from the tangle of bushes, fallen trees, and wet grass. One is well-muscled and wearing a green leather jacket. The other, smaller, is wearing a black T-shirt. They give us a hard look. A tough-guy look. The muscular one reaches into his jacket. It's a move intended to tell us that he's got something in there.

Solo presses his foot on the accelerator. The car—our car, the one I'm sitting in—smashes straight into the Miata. Right into its driver's-side door panel.

The impact jolts me hard against my shoulder belt. But it's not enough to pop the airbag.

"Hey!" I yell. Because what else is there to yell when someone deliberately crashes a car?

Both guys stare, jaws open. A cigarette falls.

"Whoa! Sorry!" Solo says, and it's a very convincing apology.

"What the—" Leather Jacket yells and stabs the air with his cigarette.

"Sorry, man, sorry!" Solo yells. He whips out his phone and starts dialing. "I'm all over 911. My bad. Totally my bad. But we need the cops to come so I can report it."

"No cops," Leather Jacket says. He shakes a no-no finger at Solo.

"Gotta have cops, bro," Solo says. I don't believe Solo is a guy who has ever used the word "bro" before, and I'm pretty sure he never will again. But it does the job of making him seem harmless and not very bright.

Leather Jacket pulls a gun.

I've never actually seen a gun in real life. I think it's a toy. But some part of my brain is screaming something about it being real and getting shot and oh please no and I don't want to die and no no no, even though on the outside I'm pretty sure I look calm.

"Get the hell out of here," the thug says.

This is when I learn the useful thing about electric cars: There's no roar of a gas engine when you stomp on the accelerator. Which is what Solo does, with the car in reverse and the wheel turned sharply.

The car jerks back so hard it's like we've been hit again, and for a second some confused part of my brain half wonders if I've been shot. But no: no bang noise.

The front left bumper swings back hard, right into Leather Jacket.

It's a glancing blow. Nothing like the blow that knocked my leg clean off. But there's no such thing as a love-tap when a car hits you.

Leather Jacket is down, down hard, on his back in the grass. One leg's beneath the car and his gun is on the grass behind his head.

He doesn't reach for either. He tries to sit up. It's a bad move because Solo thrusts his door open and hits him in the face with it. Down goes Leather Jacket again, and this time he's not going to get up soon.

It all happens so fast, too fast to parse out the individual actions, a blur of flash images, sudden jerks, jolts, noises, cries, crunches, the leap-back of T-shirt.

We hear shouts. Two guys are running toward us from the direction of the still-unseen lake. T-shirt is yelling, but he doesn't know what to do. The two new arrivals run, see their friend down on the ground, see us, slow down. If one of them has a gun, I tell myself, he would have pulled it out by now.

"Let your boyfriend know he can come out, it's safe," Solo instructs Aislin in an amazingly calm voice.

I turn to see if she's okay. Her fingers are trembling as she tries to text.

The car is still in reverse. Solo eases it backward until the left front wheel encounters an obstacle. It's Leather's leg.

Solo says, "We're here to pick up our friend. If you let him through, no problem. If you don't, then I'm going to back right over your friend's leg."

Maddox appears. He's soaking wet, muddy from his sneakers to his chest. Dead leaves and sticks cling to him like a half-hearted attempt at camouflage.

He's a good-looking guy, Maddox is, in a hulky, fullback kind of way. Although right now, terrified and soggy, he just looks pathetic.

"Get in!" Aislin yells.

Solo waits until he's buckled up. "Pull your boy out from

under and call an ambulance," he instructs the three glaring thugs.

"Everyone ready?"

Oh, we're ready.

We pull away and Solo says, "It's so much easier when you don't have to worry about surveillance cameras."

Maddox hugs Aislin like a drowning man grabbing the last life preserver. She tolerates it for a few seconds, then punches him in the chest and pushes him away.

"Hey!"

"Dumbass!" she screams.

I'm ignoring them because I can't stop staring at Solo, who is driving away with quiet competence, merging into traffic and turning into the Sunset District.

"How did you . . . ," I begin, but I don't really know how to finish the question.

He emits a short bark of a laugh. "The rat who runs the maze every day develops some moves. And I am the boss rat."

It's not a joke. He tries to pretend it is, but there's something there, seething beneath the surface.

We drive in silence. At least the front seat is silent. Aislin and Maddox are alternately yelling and making out.

"I have to get the car back," Solo says. "There's a short window of time."

I twist around in my seat. "Aislin, you need to come with me."

"She's going with me," Maddox says. He's sullen, not his usual charming self. Really, he is charming. But not when he's scared and muddy and shaky with the aftereffects of adrenaline, I guess.

I know, because I'm shaky myself. I didn't actually have time to be scared. The whole mess lasted maybe a minute or two.

No more. Now I'm scared. Scared and pissed.

"Damn you, Maddox!" I rage. "You could have gotten us all killed."

"No way," he protests, but it's weak. "They would have just beaten the hell out of me."

"Yeah, because nothing like that ever gets out of control," I shout. "Solo saved your butt, you loser." I'm on a roll now. "Get out of Aislin's life and stop dragging her down with you."

Aislin looks out the window at the lights streaking past. Not at me, not at Maddox.

"I can't sneak them back into Spiker," Solo says. "There are limits to my maze rat powers."

"I can get Aislin in. Right through the front door," I reply.

Solo shakes his head slightly. "Not without some explanation for how she got there. We need to drop her first. After we're back, then we can get her in."

"Aislin, we'll drop you off at your house," I say. "Or wherever you want. But you have to get a cab and come to Spiker. Stay with me for a while. At least until your parents get back from Barbados."

"Belize."

Aislin's parents travel a lot. They are perpetually tan.

"Hey, I still have a few days of school and—"

"Dammit, Aislin!" I yell, cutting her off. "We can get you to school."

"Sweetheart," she says, reaching over to put her hand on my arm. She gives me the look I secretly think of as her "doomed" look. It's the weary, knowing, sad look that says, *I'm a bad seed, I'm unlucky in life, this is my fate, and you can't really help me.*

That's all she says. Just "sweetheart."

I turn away, angry. I tell Solo to drop Aislin and Maddox at her parents' place.

What is it that gets inside a person and convinces them to self-destruct? Is it their home life? Sometimes. But Aislin's home life isn't terrible. Her parents fight, but so do lots of people's parents. They're not rich, but they have enough money, enough, anyway, to get her into our snooty private school. Enough to keep their tans fresh.

Her mother is kind of a weak, ditzy, and inconsequential woman—the polar opposite of my mother. Absolutely no one has ever described Terra Spiker as weak. But it's not like Aislin is being abused. I would know. We have no secrets. Her father is just like Aislin, a funny, charming, and, um, shall we say, adventurous person. But he loves Aislin and she knows it.

They're distracted parents, not always around, not perfect. Join the club.

So what's the deal?

Is it all just DNA? Is that twisted double helix the all-controlling code we can never outwit? Is there some chromosome deep down in Aislin's cells that dooms her to a life of unhappiness with losers like Maddox?

On the other hand, Aislin, at least, has a relationship.

Oh, that was a cruel shot from my own brain. I'm actually arguing with myself as we motor through the streets, looking for Aislin's house.

Yes, she has a relationship. A bad relationship.

Is a bad relationship supposed to be better than none at all?

How would you know?

There's no hurry. I'm not a pint of half-and-half about to expire. I can wait until I meet the right person.

You mean the perfect person. The flawless person. That person doesn't exist.

We drop Aislin. I beckon her to my window, and in a loud whisper that Maddox, to his credit, pretends not to hear, I tell her to come straight to Spiker and stay with me. I beg and plead and know I'm wasting my time.

I watch Aislin and Maddox head inside. She waves wanly before closing the door.

I slam The Leg against the dashboard. "Oh, she drives me crazy sometimes."

"Your leg doesn't seem to be bothering you at all," Solo notes.

"What?" He's right. I'd forgotten all about it. "Yeah, well, that's not my main worry right now."

He holds my gaze as if waiting for something. I have the sudden, bizarre thought that he might be thinking about kissing me.

"Not even," I say. "I didn't suddenly turn vulnerable to your charm."

His eyebrows rise. "Oh, you thought I was going to make a move on you?"

"I didn't—" I start to say, retreating.

"Stop projecting your feelings on me," Solo says.

It's a breathtakingly effective put-down.

I can't think of a single thing to say in response, although I'm pretty sure I'll have something in about three hours, when it's too late to matter.

"No, I thought maybe things were starting to connect for you, that was all," Solo says as he pulls the car out. "Of course, if you insist on throwing yourself at me, I guess I could play along."

"There will be no throwing."

"Well, it's going to have to come from you," he says. "You're the boss's daughter. You'll have to make the first move."

"Then consider yourself safe," I say.

I turn on the radio.

Loud.

17

SNEAKING BACK IN IS EASIER THAN I IMAGINED. STILL, THE WHOLE THING'S LEFT me feeling agitated, tired, confused.

Solo rolls me to the clinic, where they've apparently been a bit frantic, what with having misplaced the boss's daughter. Fortunately, my mother's been at the spa all day. She is unreachable when she's being detoxified, rejuvenated, or antiaged.

"I was just touring the place," I assure Dr. Anderson.

"You should be in bed," he chides. "You are in no condition to be touring."

Or chasing down gangbangers, I add silently.

Once the staff is properly reassured, Solo wheels me to the workstation where Project 88715 is set up. I've begun to think of it as "my" workstation. My project.

The overhead lights are dimmed, but the twinkle lights on the giant ficus are lit. No one's around.

I clear my throat. "Thanks," I say. "For helping with Aislin."

"No problem." Solo shoves his hands in his pockets. "Hey, you hungry? I can run down to the cafeteria, see what's lying around."

"No, I'm good. Too wired."

"You think Aislin will show up?"

"No," I say. "I can't compete with Maddox's allure."

Solo laughs, stares at his shoes. "You're all right. But you're no Maddox."

The tension in the car seems to have passed. Good. We can pretend it never happened.

I sign in, tap a few keys, and suddenly, a giant pair of blue eyes—Solo's eyes—float before us. "Adam awaits," I say.

"Adam, huh?"

"That's what Aislin named him. Could be Steve, though. Work in progress."

Solo locks my wheelchair into place. "Okay, then," he says. "Night."

"Night. And thanks again."

I feel strangely alone when he's gone. Various machines hum softly, but otherwise, it's utterly quiet.

The eyes throb gently, casting a blue moon glow over my desk.

I should probably work on the rest of Adam's face. Those eyes need a home, after all.

I consult the screen, scanning my options. The software gives me a little flexibility. After a few minutes of hesitation, I click "hands."

I don't know why. I tell myself it's because opposable thumbs are so important to Homo sapiens. Tool use and all that.

It sounds profound in my head.

The face? That's just cosmetics, really. Hands, though, well, hands *do* things. Hands create.

I'm getting pretty good with the software now. When it flashes a warning to me about blood supply, I remember how to hook the virtual hands to the temporary virtual blood supply. The software shifts view subtly, just as it did with the eyes, and the hands assume an eerie reality.

Hands. With tubes streaming blood back and forth.

Hands, floating in a medium of some sort, approximately two and a half feet below the eyes which, likewise, float in nothingness.

I have hands. Nice hands. And a pair of eyeballs. Nice eyeballs.

All that's left is a face, legs, arms, shoulders, chest, back, and a brain.

Yes. That's all of it. Or him.

I fidget a little. Why am I reluctant to give him a face?

Because, really, how do you do a face? That's why. That's part of it, anyway.

There's something else, though. Once you have a face you have a person. A specific individual.

Adam won't be Adam until he has a face.

And he won't get a face until I design one.

I chew on my lower lip. Okay, then.

Brow. Shouldn't be low, I don't like low brows. I don't want it too high, just higher than average.

Where there's a brow, there's hair. Blond? Brunette? Redhead? Rupert Grint has red hair. He seems nice.

Am I looking for nice?

No. Not Rupert nice. A little less nice.

Daniel Craig. He has blond hair. He may be nice in real life, but he doesn't play nice in the movies. Blond can be cruel.

"This is idiotic," I say.

"What is?"

I jump. I don't know the voice. I spin around and see an extremely strange person. He appears to be tattooed everywhere except his face. No, scratch that: He has a tattoo on his brow. Speaking of brows.

"What's idiotic?" he demands sharply.

"Who are you?"

"I happen to be Dr. Holyfield. I'm in charge of Project 88715."

"Oh."

"I would like to know what's idiotic."

I'm not intimidated. He wants me to be, he's frowning, but I'm not easily intimidated. Certainly not in a building with my family's name on the outside.

"Hair. I was debating hair color," I explain.

He stares at me like he can't accept my answer. Like there must be a better answer that I'm just refusing to tell him.

I hold his gaze.

He doesn't like that, either. Too bad.

"Hair color is irrelevant," he says at last. "It's nothing but aesthetics. That's not why you're running this simulation. Your mother didn't task you to discover your preferences in hair color."

"Huh. Then why did she 'task' me?"

"Because she wants to keep you occupied, I assume." He shrugs when I fail to take offense. "And, I suppose, because it might be informative to see what an ordinary person comes up with."

"Ordinary."

He stares at my work so far—eyeballs and hands. "Why would you start with hands and eyes?"

I take a deep breath. The truth is, I haven't spent much time thinking about the "why." But I don't want to admit it. This guy is annoying me. Set aside the tattoos, and he's like a lot of the other Spiker scientists I've been introduced to: arrogant and in love with his own IQ.

So I say, "Because gods want to be seen, and they want to be served."

"Gods?"

I lift my shoulders in what I hope is a parody of his *too cool for school* attitude. "Don't give me the job of creating a human unless you want me to have delusions of God-hood."

"It's just a sim," he says, and his eyes narrow suspiciously.

"Okay, and I'm just a God sim."

The conversation is not going his way. "If there were a God in this process, it would be the guy who created the RDSS-3 software and married it up to the CGMs."

"The what?"

"The Rapid DNA Selection System and of course the Controlled . . ." He stops, glares, and actually thumps his chest. "Me. That's who designed the RDSS and realized its potential."

"So *you're* God."

He snorts. "Well, you're not. I designed this system. You're just using it."

"Yeah. Like an artist uses paint. Right?" I ask it innocently. "I'll bet the guy who sold Da Vinci paint thought *he* was the artist."

"Mmm," he says, his eyes hard. "It must be nice to be you, kid. Rich and privileged. Everything handed to you on a silver platter. Must be very nice."

He turns on his heel and walks away.

What on earth is a CGM? I wonder. Controlled . . . That's as far as he got, and then he stopped himself.

I Google it. CGM and the word "controlled." Plenty of results, none of them very interesting.

"Dark hair," I say to no one.

Dark hair it is. I tap the screen, I move the jelly beans. But the program informs me that I have made an error. We're going to need a scalp and an entire head before we can grow hair.

I have no idea how to decide on a head shape. In my entire life I've never spent three seconds thinking about head shapes.

I get back on Google and start educating myself.

"Wait a minute," I mutter aloud. "Is that what she's up to?" Is my mother trying to entice me into majoring in genetics? Nah, that would be too motherly, not sufficiently subterranean.

Hmm.

It doesn't matter, anyway. I'm enjoying this. And it's a good way to take my mind off Aislin and Solo and The Leg.

For the next three hours I barely look up from the screen.

And when at last I do look up, there's Adam, looking back at me.

He has a very handsome face. The nose is perfect. The cheekbones could belong to a male model. The black hair is lush and lustrous. The mouth . . . that's the only thing I'm not entirely happy with. That mouth, those lips, are almost too perfect. There's something unnerving about a perfectly shaped mouth.

The eyes are blank, no glimmer of intelligence or thought or awareness behind them.

And suddenly I realize that I was right in my glib answer to Dr. Holyfield. I want my creation to see me.

For that, I will have to give Adam a brain.

– 18 –

SOLO

MY PHONE GOES OFF AT 2:14 A.M.

I roll out of bed, stand up, realize the phone is still ringing, turn around, try to remember where the hell the phone is and what the hell it would be doing ringing. I find it and fumble with it and hold it the wrong way to my head.

I don't wake up well at two in the morning.

"Solo."

My eyes widen. It's Terror her own self. At 2:14 in the morning. And suddenly I am acutely aware of the fact that I am not dressed, not at all, and without meaning to I glance toward where the security camera is.

I don't worry about walking around naked. First, ninety-nine percent of security footage is never seen by anyone. It just goes straight into the servers. And second, on those rare occasions when camera footage is played, it's for a bored security guy.

Anyway, I just don't have much of a modesty thing.

Unless it's Herself, the Mighty One, the Evil Queen herself, calling me in the middle of the night.

"Yeah?" I say, because it's all I can come up with.

"I need you. Be at the south elevator, Level Two."

"When?"

"Now."

"Now?"

"Am I stuttering? Now."

I hesitate, trying to get the processors up to speed.

"I've already called two other employees, both of whom were unable or unwilling to respond. Both of whom are now former employees."

"I'm on my way," I say.

Click.

"What the hell?" I ask my room. I feel perfectly and completely awake and yet I manage to pull my jeans on backward anyway. And where did I leave my shirt? Does it smell? Are there clean ones in my closet? Yes, there's one.

Find the front of the shirt. Okay. Good. Shoes.

I'm more or less dressed and I barrel out into the hallway, bleary, hair all over the place, no socks, underwear, or belt. My left eye has apparently been glued shut, but I am on the move.

I reach the elevator and ride it down to the second floor, which is the main reception area. Elevators coming from the parking garage come here first. It's an amazingly impressive, intimidating space, a soaring four-story-tall atrium with a massive double helix floating in the air, all glowing colors and soft pulsations.

The lights are down, with soft spots on the elevator doors and the sweep of the reception desk. There's a security guy sitting there, surprised to see me. He's just thinking of asking me why I'm there when we hear the click-click of Terra's high heels.

The guard quickly straightens his tie, shoots me a look, and stands up as Terra sweeps in.

Honestly, how does she manage to be that put-together at this hour? Sure, Eve mentioned she was at a spa all day, but it's two-something in the morning and the woman looks like she just stepped off the cover of *Hot 'N' Scary Moms* magazine.

She stares hard at me, like she's caught me doing something. I flush with guilt because there are so many possibilities.

"That damned girl," she says. "She's here."

Really? She's referring to her own daughter as "that damned girl?" That seems harsh, even for Terra Spiker.

"I was in the middle of work," Terra continues.

At two in the morning? I think, but I keep my mouth shut.

"And now, you'll notice, I am not in the middle of work."

The elevator dings. The door slides open. There's a plain-clothes security guy—instantly recognizable by the MIB suit and the earpiece. And the gun bulge under his jacket.

He has a tight grip on Aislin's arm.

I start to grin at Aislin. Then I see. Her nose has been split, right across the bridge. One eye is red and puffy and will soon be black. There's a welt on her neck, a shoulder strap that was obviously torn and then retied hastily. There's blood on a patch of scalp where someone has torn her hair out.

The guard and Aislin step off the elevator. He's still holding her arm in his big fist like she's a threat.

"What a surprise to see you, Aislin," Terra says in a voice that could freeze oxygen.

For once Aislin is at a loss for words. She's been crying. She sees Terra, winces, and her eyes slide over to find me. For a second there's a look of total vulnerability. It's hard to see: She's not the vulnerable type.

"A surprise to see you, not a surprise to see you in trouble," Terra says. "And you wonder why I don't want my daughter dealing with you? Look at yourself."

"Leave her alone." The words are out of my mouth before I know it.

Both security guys suffer simultaneous heart attacks. No one breathes. Terra glares incredulously at me. I see a faintly amused look in Aislin's eyes. And gratitude.

Terra lets it go after no more than a single sharp intake of breath. "Aislin will be spending the night, Solo," she says. "Find her a room. Do not wake Evening. She's still recuperating and doesn't need . . . this."

The word "this" is drenched in venom.

"Twenty-four hours," Terra tells Aislin, manicured finger puncturing the air. "And only because my daughter would hate me if I didn't."

She clickety-clacks ten paces away, stops, half-turns, and says, "And page Dr. Anderson, Solo. The girl's a mess."

And then she vanishes.

"Hey, Solo," Aislin says sheepishly, as the guard walks away.

"Let's go get Eve," I say.

"No, no, no, you heard her mom."

"Yeah, well, Terra can go . . . she can drop dead. Something bad happened with you. You came here to see Eve, not me."

She half-leans against me. She smells like booze and cigarettes. "You're a good guy. I hope E.V. figures that out."

I ignore her.

No, I don't exactly ignore her. It's more like an arrow's been shot into my chest and I find myself kind of startled and breathless and, I don't know, I don't know what that other emotion is. Like something I didn't know was in me, and then suddenly there it is.

I walk Aislin down the hallway. She's leaning on me and she's wobbly but I don't think it's from drink. I think she's holding on by her fingernails.

"Did you call the cops?"

"Long story," she says.

"Because you should—"

We pass the nurses' station. "We're going to see Eve," I say. "Evening."

The nurse leaps to her feet. "That girl needs attention."

"Page Dr. Anderson," I say.

"I'm good," Aislin says, waving her hand vaguely.

Eve's door is open, but I knock anyway. It takes a couple rounds before she wakes up.

"Yeah?" she calls.

"It's Solo. I'm with Aislin."

"What?"

"Hi, E.V.," Aislin calls.

"What . . . just come in, will you?"

Eve looks about like I probably looked twenty minutes ago. Like she can only open one eye. And there's possible drool in the left corner of her mouth.

Why do I find that kind of hot? Seriously. Sleep drool.

She sits up. She's wearing a too-small T-shirt. Her hair is all on one side of her head.

Her eyes widen. She barely notices me. Aislin staggers over to the bed and just sort of melts into her arms. It's a long hug. I stand in the doorway, staring at my feet.

I'm thinking it's time for me to sneak away quietly when Eve looks at me over Aislin's shoulder, frowns, and jerks her head a little, indicating that I should come in.

I do. Feeling like I'm entering the Holy of Holies.

Oh my God. I've never been in a girl's room before. It smells different in here. It smells good.

Still, the realization is disheartening somehow. All of this is new to me. Including the acknowledgment that it's all new to me.

"Aislin," Eve says softly. "Oh, Aislin."

The nurse appears in the doorway. "Dr. Anderson's on his

way," she says. "And you're in no condition to be having visitors in the middle of the night."

"Please," Eve says, stroking Aislin's hair, "leave us."

The nurse wrings her hands.

"Two minutes," Eve snaps, and the nurse retreats.

There's some of her mother in Eve, I realize with a shock. I've never seen it in her before, but when she wants to, Eve can summon up that same voice of command and control.

"So?" Eve asks Aislin.

Aislin won't meet her eyes.

Eve looks at me. I start answering before I realize I'm doing it.

"Your mother woke me, told me to meet her at the elevator. Aislin came up. I'm supposed to find her a place to stay."

Eve hears what I didn't say. "My mother told you to bring her here, to me?"

"No. Actually she told me absolutely not to do that."

Eve's forbidding expression softens.

"I don't always do exactly what I'm told," I say.

"Well, thanks," she says.

I comb my fingers through my hair. It's tangled up, even by my standards, which are pretty low. "I should get going."

"Stay," Eve says firmly, going all Terra on me again. She winces, looks down, smiles a little. "I mean, please stay, if you don't mind."

I grab a chair. "Sure. No problem." I was hoping she'd say that.

"Tell me, Aislin," Eve says gently.

"They came to Maddox's apartment." Aislin takes a shuddery

breath. "I was there. They started banging. Crazy. Threatening him. They broke a window and someone must have called the cops. Which was lucky because they got in. The gangbangers, not the cops, I mean. I tried to . . . so one of them . . ." She mimes a punch. She started strong, but now the narrative is breaking up. She's breathing hard, as if the whole thing's happening all over again.

"The guy, so he hit me, and I fell down. Kicked me in . . . Maddox, they had him, the other guys, and they were tying him down. He was yelling for help. I tried. My phone. Then, wham again. A gun and they were pointing it. Maddox. Then the sirens and I ran, I got out of the door and down the stairs and I was going to get the cops to come and help. Confused, because of being hit and all."

Eve looks at me.

There's a knock on Eve's door. It's Dr. Anderson with the nurse, who's carrying a tray of bandages and sutures.

"Jeez," the doctor says. He is wearing a pair of red silk pajamas. His feet are bare.

Dr. Anderson moves Aislin to a spot where the light is better, over by the desk. He peers sideways at her nose. The cut looks bad. The nurse tsk-tsks under her breath.

The doctor pulls on rubber gloves, prodding the wound. "Yep. It'll definitely need stitches, young lady. But first let's get a radiograph, make sure nothing's broken."

Aislin doesn't complain. She's kind of gone somewhere else in her head.

The nurse and doctor help her out the door. "It'll only take a minute," the nurse says.

"You stay put," Dr. Anderson admonishes Eve. "You've had enough fun for one day."

"It wasn't all fun," I offer.

Eve presses her lips together, suppressing a smile.

"Should I go?" I ask Eve when they've left. "I mean, there's nothing more I can do, I guess."

Eve adjusts her sheets. "It'd be okay if you stick around," she says casually. I can't tell if she wants me around or not. "I might need backup while I'm reading Aislin the riot act."

"Yeah, okay," I say, matching her tone. "I'm totally wide awake, anyway."

We sit in silence. The mirror has get-well cards taped to it. There are flowers everywhere. Girl things are scattered around the room: a makeup kit, a bottle of perfume, something unidentifiable that's beige and silky.

Aislin returns with the nurse and doctor. "Nothing broken," he reports. "Think we can put Humpty Dumpty together again." He yawns widely. "Nurse, you can finish up. The Ambien's kicking in again."

Aislin settles in a leather chair as the nurse prepares her equipment.

"Listen, sweetie," Eve begins in a lecturing voice. She hears it herself and I can see it makes her uncomfortable. But she has to go on. I want her to go on. Someone has got to tell Aislin what's what.

"This has to stop, Aislin. You know it. I know it. The whole world knows it. You're going to end up hurt."

"It'll be okay," Aislin says. But there's no force to her words. She doesn't believe what she's saying.

"I know you care about Maddox," Eve says. "But this can't go on."

"I'm going to numb you up," the nurse says.

Aislin is crying. I don't think it's from pain.

Before long the nurse leaves. Aislin's nose looks a little like Eve's leg. It's a mess of white bandages.

Aislin gets up to examine herself in the mirror. "Ugh, how long do I have to look like this?"

"Look how fast my face healed up," Eve offers.

"It's going to take Aislin a lot longer than it took you," I say. It's out of my mouth. Too late to call it back now. For a second I think no one will say anything.

"Why should it take her longer?" Eve asks. It's like I've dissed Aislin.

I don't answer. I hang my head, elbows on my knees.

"Solo?" Eve presses. "Why aren't you answering me?"

I look up through my eyebrows. I look pointedly at the bathroom. "In there." I mouth the words soundlessly.

To my relief, both of them catch on immediately.

"Can you grab my wheelchair?" Eve asks me.

"Try standing," I suggest.

She gives me a skeptical frown. "Are you kidding? No way."

"Okay, then. I'll play crutch," I say, shrugging. Like it's a hardship.

I slip my arm around Eve and help her hobble into the bathroom. Aislin follows, moving unsteadily.

With the door closed, it's cramped but not too bad: The suite is roomy and so is the bathroom. I rummage in the medicine cabinet, then in the drawers. I pull out a pair of scissors.

"What are you doing?" Eve asks.

I kneel in front of her. "Which is easier? Hike up or drop trou?"

She sees what I'm getting at. With a rather baleful expression on her face, Eve slides the pajama bottoms down. They puddle around her ankles.

"That's what you wear for panties?" Aislin protests.

"They're comfortable."

I have no comment. I am content to swallow hard.

The thick bandages extend from her ankle to her upper thigh. Her upper, upper thigh. Very carefully, hands trembling, I pull the edge of the bandage away from her thigh and insert the scissors, point down.

Aislin runs her index finger along her bandaged nose. "You know, now that I think about it, it's weird, the way they didn't give you a cast for that leg."

"Actually, it's not so weird," I say.

"What are you doing?" Eve asks. But not with any serious intent. Not like she's actually going to stop me. There's a quaver in her voice.

I cut.

Down the inside of her thigh.

I reach the place where the leg was severed. I roll the bandage down to expose it.

The three of us stare.

The bathroom light is unforgiving.

Where her leg had been crudely ripped apart—skin shredded, bone snapped, muscle meat torn like a turkey drumstick—there is smooth, unblemished white skin.

19

EVƎ

"THERE ISN'T EVEN A SCAR," AISLIN MURMURS.

We all stare for a while. I extend shaking fingers toward my leg.

I need to touch to believe.

The skin isn't even bumpy. It's not just smooth. It's absolutely identical to the way it was before the accident.

I push the bandages down farther. It's like taking off a very tight legging. All the way to my knee, just in case, just in case memory is playing some weird trick on me.

"We're awake, right?" I ask.

Solo stands up. He sets the scissors on the counter. "It's been like this for days. By the second day everything was fine. By the third day the scars would have already been disappearing. Day four?" He lifts his shoulders. "There can be variations, it's not an exact thing."

Aislin seems to have forgotten her own injuries. "That's not possible. Is it?"

"Solo," I say. He has the answers. I can tell.

"Have you ever had a scrape or a skinned knee that lasted more than a day?" he asks.

"Um . . . I don't know." I scroll back over a lifetime of Band-Aids. "Who keeps track?"

"Cuts? Bruises?" Solo leans back against the sink, arms crossed over his chest. "Toothaches?"

"I'm an excellent flosser," I say defensively.

"Colds? Flu?"

My heart is hammering. "I use Purell?" I say with a weak smile. "How many colds have you had in your life?"

Solo tenses. He starts to say something, then catches himself. "We're talking about you."

"She never gets sick," Aislin says softly. "Like . . . never. She doesn't even get cramps."

I shoot her a look.

She holds up her hands in a placating gesture. "Well, it's true."

"So I'm the picture of health. I'm lucky," I say. Gingerly I touch my thigh.

Solo shakes his head. "No one is that lucky."

"Wait! I know!" I cry triumphantly. "When I was around two I had heart surgery." I am weirdly relieved by this fact. "It was some valve thing. Congenital. They repaired it, though. With pig tissue, actually."

Aislin frowns. "Like . . . bacon?"

"No," Solo says to me. "They didn't repair it surgically."

"Obviously, they did. Because here I am, fine. Beyond fine."
I chew on a thumbnail, considering. "And how could you possibly
know what happened when I was two, anyway?"

Solo looks at his feet. "You didn't have long to live, Eve," he
says. "The odds of getting a heart transplant were pretty slim. At
some level, you can see why they did it. They were desperate."

I grab his arm. "What are you telling me?"

"You're a mod." Solo touches my hand and I loosen my grip
on his arm. "You're genetically modified. It happened when you
were two. It's in your file."

He waits while I absorb this.

I leave him waiting.

I am not absorbing.

"Two days after your surgery, you were completely cured," Solo
says. "The doctors probably thought they were seeing things. What
they were seeing was the Logan Serum. Either your mom or your
dad must have injected you."

"Logan Serum," I repeat dully.

"Cool," Aislin says, staring at her reflection in the mirror.
"Can I get some?"

"No one can get any," Solo replies. "It's never been approved
by the FDA, by the government."

"Why not, if it's so—" I start, but just then Aislin's legs buckle
just a little. She catches herself, but I can see the night has taken
a big toll.

"I need a drink of water," she says in a little girl voice.

I fill a glass from the tap. Solo catches Aislin as she suddenly folds up. He lifts her easily. She's not unconscious, just in that strange zone between awake and asleep.

Solo places her on my bed. I put a pillow under her head, pull off her boots, and cover her with a blanket.

I motion Solo to follow me back into the bathroom. The Leg is surprisingly limber, but my hands won't stop trembling.

I shut the bathroom door. "First of all, we're in here because there aren't any surveillance cameras, right?"

"Yes."

"This thing." I toy with the sink handle. I don't want to look directly at Solo. "This healing thing. Why doesn't everyone have it? I mean, why doesn't my mother, why doesn't Spiker . . ."

"Because it's illegal. The way they made it was illegal. They took shortcuts with human testing. Now they have to re-create the whole thing from scratch, pretending to discover it and test it the right way. That takes years."

I force myself to look at him.

There's more. I can see it in his eyes. I can see that he's challenging me to ask. I can see that he's almost eager to tell me.

That's what makes me hold off. I don't want to hear any more. Not now. Not yet.

It's one thing to know that your mother skirts the law from time to time. My mother's always been in the gray zone when it comes to ethics.

It's another thing altogether to know that your mother

broke the law outright. And that she did it in order to save your life.

It seems like something she might have mentioned, oh, I don't know, over breakfast one morning: *Make yourself an Eggo, Evening, and don't forget your science project. Hey, speaking of science projects, Daddy and I had you genetically modified when you were two. Please put your dishes in the sink.*

Solo knows I don't want to know. He laughs, a hard, flat sound. He opens the bathroom door and crosses my room. "I gotta go. I'm beat. If your mom asks, Aislin found her own way here." He pulls a key card out of his back pocket. "This is for Suite Fourteen. That's supposed to be her room."

I take the key. I have to say thanks, don't I? He risked a lot, bringing Aislin to me.

But somehow the word doesn't come from my mouth. All I can say is, "Good night," and he's gone.

Aislin snores.

* * *

DESPITE EVERYTHING, I SLEEP. DESPITE AISLIN'S HAND THROWN ACROSS MY FACE. Despite the strangely detailed memories of dropping my pajamas to the floor while Solo is at eye level with my unsexy panties.

The sense memory, the shiver that comes with it, of Solo running careful fingers down my inner thigh.

Despite all of that, I sleep. I dream of a hospital. But not the one here at Spiker. Or the emergency room.

131

It's a hospital room far back in my past.

I see my mother. I see my dad.

I dream of my father sometimes, never of my mother.

But in this dream, they're together, whispering. My mother is holding a syringe. My father nods his approval. They are both crying.

I wake up to a blast of very bad breath from Aislin. She smells of puke. I hope she made it to the bathroom. I stagger up and find the toilet bowl full. Well, better than the bed.

My bandage is flapping loosely. I either have to cut it all the way off, or try to conceal my guilty knowledge until my next scheduled bandage-change.

It hits me then, what should have hit me earlier: They're all in on it. The doctors, the nurses. They know the injury's gone.

They're all in on it. All playing a game, hiding the truth from me.

It's why my mother was in such a hurry to get me out of the hospital and safely to Spiker. My secret would have been out within a day. And what would have happened to my mother if it had come out that she'd broken the law? Many laws?

It's dark in the room but the clock shows 8:42 A.M. I would normally be up by now. I'm buzzy from lack of sleep, and my head is full of pictures and words. Aislin's bloody face. The dream memory of a long-ago hospital room. Solo's words: *You're a mod. You're genetically modified.* The unreal sensation of my fingertips on the place where terrible damage should be.

Despite this, what I remember most is Solo kneeling on the bathroom floor.

I head for the bathroom. Aislin snores softly.

I grab the scissors Solo used to cut off my leg bandage. Awkwardly, I slit the bandages on my right arm and hand.

I bend my crushed fingers, wave my mangled hand, flex my broken elbow.

It's as if nothing ever happened.

You're genetically modified.

Don't think about it.

I take a hot, hot shower. I can't believe how good it feels. Standing upright in the stinging spray is a gift. Shampooing my hair with both hands is bliss.

I towel off, change into fresh clothes, actual jeans with two legs. Then I reach—with my right hand, no less—for my sketchbook and pencil.

Don't think about it. Don't think about it.

I open to the unfinished sketch I'd been working on for Life Drawing.

The pencil feels smooth and certain between my fingers. The whispered resistance of point on paper is music.

I make a few random lines, just to get the rhythm right.

Don't think about it.

I study my drawing. It still sucks.

It needs something. Energy, spark, soul.

Life drawing, my ass. This is a still life.

It's the eyes. The eyes are all wrong. They're nothing like the eyes I've been creating with the aid of my mother's software.

Adam's eyes pulse with possibilities.

These eyes . . . well, they're granules of graphite on recycled wood product.

Don't think about it.

I start to erase the left eye, but suddenly I picture the dog-eared poster on the art room wall: "Creativity is allowing yourself to make mistakes. Art is knowing which ones to keep."

I turn to a new page, tear it out, and write Aislin a quick note.

I put the paper by her pillow. She's kicked off her blankets, so I tuck them around her chin. Her cheek looks like an overripe plum, purple-black and swollen.

I stash my sketchbook in a drawer.

Then I flee for the safety of Adam.

20

I SETTLE INTO MY WORKSTATION. A SHAFT OF SUNLIGHT SLICES THE AIR. THE twinkling ficus tree has dropped a leaf onto my keyboard. A couple of workers glance up when I appear, then quickly return to their monitors.

I enter my password. Click, click, tap, tap.

I can type again. Two hands, ten fingers.

Adam materializes.

He is a good-looking guy, Adam. Very good-looking.

Apparently, the other workers think so, too. They stare, as if hypnotized, at his hovering form.

"I want her job," someone murmurs.

I glance over, and, in perfect sync, all gazes return to their respective monitors. I am, after all, Terra Spiker's daughter: Eye contact is not an option.

Terra Spiker, who's apparently capable of anything.

I wiggle the fingers of my right hand. My perfect, pain-free fingers.

They were trying to save my life. They *did* save my life.

If they hadn't cut corners, ignored the FDA, I wouldn't be here.

Wouldn't I do the same thing for someone I love? For Aislin?

Yep. In a heartbeat.

But would I have kept it a secret from her, a secret she has to hear from some stranger?

Solo's not a stranger, some part of my brain protests. But he is, of course. I know virtually nothing about him, except that he hates my mother.

Click, click. I focus on the monitor.

I realize that Adam's eyes—which, yes, happen to be the color of Solo's, which, yes, is just a coincidence—aren't as lifelike as I'd remembered.

Like my sketch, the gaze is blank. There's an emptiness, a void. Still, there's a feeling of, I don't know, *possibility* with Adam.

This isn't like art. I know how to fix this problem.

The set of tools for designing the genetic components of the brain are different. They aren't as simple as the first steps in creation: Plug in this gene and presto, you've got blue eyes or dark hair or lungs.

I scan the instructions. They make clear, in a playful, user-friendly way, that genes may lay the table for the brain, but they don't cook the meal. Brains are about experience, too. And even at the genetic level, the interactions are so subtle and so inter-twined that you can never be sure what you're getting. The brain is a tangle of wires, billions and billions of wires, with some areas relatively sparse and other areas so densely packed that the connections seem to fuse, creating something greater than the mere connection of wires.

I scratch my wrist, where a scrap of surgical tape has been left behind. It itches. My whole body's on edge, the way I feel when I haven't been able to run for a few days.

Come to think of it, maybe that's the problem.

No, I tell myself, that's not the problem. The problem is that one way or another, you're going to have to confront your mother and tell her you know the truth.

Don't think about it. Not yet.

I could give Adam a genius-level IQ. I could drag certain icons together and come up with a massively complex brain. One that's capable of absorbing incredible detail and synthesizing vast quantities of data.

On the other hand, I might also create a person so smart he can't relate to anyone but people like himself. I could reduce his potential pool of friends, peers, lovers, to one ten-thousandth of one percent of the human race.

I could make it impossible for him to be happy.

Maybe I should make him average. He would have a wide choice of friends and possible lovers. But he'd have to work harder at school. Things might not come quite as easily to him.

He might be happier. But merely making him average wouldn't ensure that.

I could tilt him toward the arts. I could prepare him for a life of science. I could code him to be a humanitarian.

I could make him fearful and cautious. He would probably

live longer. But he might not find what he was looking for and needed.

I could make him reckless and bold. He might die younger. He might be a criminal. He might be a great creative mind.

This is not the simple, fun art work of making a face and a body. I'm not religious, but I'm starting to have some sympathy for God. Give man a brain smart enough to name the animals, one generally useful and productive, and you have to see the whole forbidden apple thing coming down the pike.

This isn't as easy as it looks.

I think about brains I've known. Aislin. What the hell is going on in her brain? She's not as book-smart as I am, and maybe that gets her into trouble. But at the same time, if you added up all the sheer pleasure and fun we've each had? Aislin's pile would look like a skyscraper next to my three-story townhouse.

And what about my mother? She's brilliant. Ambitious. Amoral.

You're a mod. You're genetically modified.

I can still hear the way Solo said it: *a mod.* As if that's a regular word, an entry in Webster's.

He sounded like a doctor when he told me. A doctor telling his patient she has an incurable illness.

Which is funny, when you think about it, because what I have amounts to a superpower. I can heal with a speed and completeness that's unbelievable. I could be a comic book hero.

And yet I never noticed.

How smart can I be if I never even noticed?

"He's . . . beautiful."

I turn to see Aislin, pointing to Adam. She's a disaster. Bruises all over one half of her face. The bandages covering the sutures are stained with seeping blood, now dried to a rust color.

She is not a mod.

"How are you feeling?" I ask. I don't get up and hug her, although I think maybe I should. I don't.

She doesn't answer. Her mouth is hanging open. "Marry me, Adam. I don't care if you're missing some parts. I love you."

"Yeah, his face turned out pretty well," I say flatly. "So again: How are you?"

Aislin tries to focus. "I'm way hungover. Plus I guess someone must have dropped a safe on me." She smiles, wincing, and I see a jagged, broken tooth.

When I was seven I broke a tooth after missing a landing on the balance beam. It grew back. How did I not notice how strange that was?

I am silent. Aislin's lower lip trembles. She is about to cry.

I stand, push back my chair. And I hug her.

Why don't I want to? Why do I feel as if my skin has been sandpapered and now everything is just too much?

"I have to help Maddox," she says into my neck.

I push her, hold her out at arm's length. "Maddox is a drug dealer. A stupid one, no less. He's a drug dealer who ripped off other drug dealers. And he got you hurt."

She steps back away from me. "What am I supposed to do? Just let them kill him?"

"How about calling the cops?"

She sighs. "He'll go to prison."

"Probably."

I tap my foot, a parody of my mother. "Aislin. Seriously. What other option do you have?"

Aislin drops into my chair. Near her part, her hair is matted with blood. "I don't know. I don't know anything anymore."

"How much does he owe?" I ask.

"I'm not asking you for money, E.V."

"How much?" There's a hard, cynical sound in my voice. I hate myself for using it.

She stares at her fingernails. "Nine thousand dollars."

I wait for Aislin to protest that she doesn't want it. That she's not asking for it. But she is, so she can't.

I don't want to do it. I shouldn't do it. But if it helps save Aislin from Maddox—from herself . . .

"If I do this, if I help out this one time, will you get your act together? Find a guy who treats you better? Will you make this crap with Maddox stop?"

Aislin sniffles, nods slightly.

The truth is, it's not much money. It's a lot for most people, but it's nothing to my mother. The only problem is, my mother doesn't give money away: She buys things. If I ask her for help, she'll own me.

But I can only be bought once. So I need to raise the price.

I pull out my phone and text my mother.

Aislin is looking at Adam. "You're missing a few parts."

"I'm working on the brain," I say, distracted.

"Why?"

"It's part of the simulation," I say. "He needs a brain. I'm trying to decide whether I should make him really smart, or just smart."

Aislin thinks for a moment. "Can you make him kind?"

My phone chimes. My mother can see me in her office in an hour.

"An hour," I report wearily, without explanation.

It's so weird. After days of longing for her company, now I want Aislin to go away.

If she senses it, she doesn't let on. "Can I watch?" she asks, pointing to Adam.

I pull an extra chair over. She sits down. We're both glum.

I show her. "See these gumdrops? What it's saying is, basically, this is a set of genes that in some other guy made him very smart. But here's a different set. And here's another set. And each of these sets, they think, made this or that person smart."

"How come they don't know?" she asks.

"Because no one quite knows. There's no single 'smart' button. It's like smart in different flavors. Smart vanilla, smart chocolate, smart raspberry."

Aislin stares intently. "You mean, they decoded some real person's DNA and figured out what made them smart? Who were the people?"

I shrug. "I don't know. The program doesn't identify them."

"So, like Einstein or Stephen Hawking?"

"Maybe."

"Well . . . that's not cool, is it? Making people who are like other people?"

"It's just a simulation," I say. "They couldn't do it in reality."

She looks at me. Her eyes are shrewd. I look away.

"Just because they did something to me . . . ," I say. I don't know the second part of the sentence.

"Are you going to ask your mom?"

"About the nine thousand?"

"About being a—what did Solo call it?—a mod."

I hold out The Limb Formerly Known As The Leg. "Let's see. I'm walking. My bandages have disappeared. I'm guessing it will come up."

We sit in silence for a while as I idly pick through brain configurations. Gradually, the tension between us bleeds away. I don't want to be distant from Aislin.

I need her. She's all I've got. And she needs me, even if she doesn't always realize it.

"We could do muscles first, then brains," Aislin suggests.

"It's not all genetic, you know: He would have to work out."

"Make him right and I'll work him out," she says with a trace of her confident leer.

"Without a brain?"

She sighs. "They're better off without one."

21

MY MOTHER'S OFFICE IS KIND OF INCREDIBLE. IT'S NOT LOW-KEY. IT'S VEGAS, baby, but with a very cool, even cold, high-tech touch.

The massive room is dominated by a thirty-foot-tall waterfall. The water runs down a series of stone planes set at angles. Very slowly, so slowly you don't notice it at first, the angles of the planes shift so that the water is always in a new configuration.

Her desk—if you can call it by so mundane a name—is a wedge of brushed stainless steel, flat where it needs to be flat, but then swooping up on the left in a way that suggests an airplane soaring into the sky, combined with a scalpel blade.

Hanging from the ceiling are sculptures my father made right before his death. He worked mostly in metal—some wood, some glass, too. These aren't mobiles, exactly. They're static sculptures suspended from cables. My father called them "airborne artifacts," sculptures meant to echo natural forms: clouds, trees, birds. My favorite, done in steel and Plexiglas, is the rough shape of a thunderbolt. There's a standing sculpture, too, one I've always loved.

It's sort of a free-form redwood tree that extends from floor to ceiling.

I don't know why my mother, who hates art, and particularly hated my father's art, has hung on to these pieces, let alone why she has them displayed. I asked her once, and she told me her interior designer needed something pretentiously ugly to fill the space.

It's a completely intimidating room. A place that says *you are nothing, and I am everything*. Somehow in the midst of all this extraordinary largeness and grandiosity, my mother still dominates.

This is not an office where you'd expect to see a cluster of corny family photos, but there they are, completely out of place, a silver-framed gallery on the wall to the right of her desk. Most are of me, a few are of my dad. One is of the three of us, the classic happy-family-on-the-beach pose.

I remember that day, a good day. Windy, too cold to venture near the water. We flew a kite until it nose-dived into the surf.

I was four, maybe five, by then. I'd already been modified. The change had long since been made.

"Hello, Evening," my mother says coolly.

"Hello."

Her eyes go to my leg. There's a flicker, but barely. "I see your leg is better."

"It's more than better. It's perfect."

She holds my gaze. I'm determined not to be the first to look away.

I look away.

"When were you going to tell me?" I ask.

"Tell you what?"

"That I'm one of your genetic experiments."

There's a long silence, during which I can hear the soft rushing of the water and the steel gears in my mother's head. Well, the water, anyway.

"I'm curious as to how you arrived at that conclusion," she says. She stands, arranging her suit, which is already perfectly arranged, and steps out from behind the Desk of Doom.

As has often been the case with my mother, I feel the urge to take a step back. But I resist.

"It's obvious," I say. "My mother runs a biotech company with a reputation for cutting corners."

She steps closer. "Would you rather have the pain? Would you rather have the scars? The lifelong limp?"

"What else have you done to me?"

She's close now. "Done to you? You mean, what other great gifts have I given you?"

"I—"

"How else have I made your life better than other people's lives? How else have I protected you?"

I'm breathing hard. Her certainty and confidence is stifling. I start to answer but my throat is dry.

Do I really want the answer?

"What is it you came for? Sweetheart?"

"I need nine thousand dollars."

"For your loser friend? I gather she found you last night? Do I have Solo to thank for that?"

I nearly panic. I can't put it on Solo. He trusted me. "She found her way to me," I say. "And she's staying. As long as she wants to."

I'm proud of the steadiness in my voice.

"Those are your demands." It's not a question. "Nine thousand dollars and a suite for your idiot BFF."

I don't see much point in quibbling about her description of Aislin. Not the time. "Yes."

"You have to stay here another week, at least," she says after a moment. "For appearances."

"Fine."

She takes a deep breath. She cocks her head, looking at me curiously, as if it's the first time she's met me. "Okay."

"Okay?"

"Okay."

"And?"

"And nothing."

Oh, she's clever. Oh, she is so very clever.

"Anything else?" she asks. Smug. She knows she's outplayed me. She knows she just bought my silence and my acceptance. For pocket change.

So that's how she got to be a billionaire.

22

SOLO

I'VE GOT TO GET THIS RIGHT.

I pause in a hallway, clenching my fists. My heart's slamming against my chest.

I've got Tattooed Tommy's poppy-seed bagel ready. What happens next will be vital. If I screw it up . . .

"Hey, Solo."

I practically leap out of my skin. It's Ben, one of the research assistants.

"Where's what's-his-name?" Ben asks. "The coffee dude."

"Jackson. He got food poisoning at the wedding. At least that's his story." I try to smile. "I'm filling in."

"Beats school, I guess."

"Barely."

Ben grabs a doughnut. He starts to leave, then, with a guilty grin, grabs another. "Big project. Carb loading."

I'm so buzzed, so exhausted, I'm wondering if I can pull this off. For the past hour I've been pushing the stupid cart around like a zombie, handing out muffins and chai tea while I answer questions in monosyllables. Grunts, practically.

I've had too little sleep, too much adrenaline.

But it's time.

I was going to wait till Eve was gone.

But something about last night, seeing her face when I told her the truth about why she'd healed so fast . . . I don't know. She won't be here much longer, and I feel like she deserves to know it all.

Maybe I just want someone else to be doing this with me. I brush the thought away.

No. That's not my style.

I wheel toward Tommy.

"Bagel boy," he says, not looking up from his screen.

His computer's in use. There's no way for me to get into it. He's added an alphanumeric password, almost as long as the one I use, backed up with retinal scan. Hack-proof, unless I can get hold of a supercomputer, ten years, and Tommy's right eyeball.

"Here's your bagel," I say.

I can see his screen. He's playing fantasy football.

Better than solitaire, I suppose.

"Any feelings on that new Jets quarterback?" he asks. His version of egalitarianism, talking to me about sports. I know nothing about sports and couldn't care less.

"Not really. Bagel?"

"No, his name's not bagel, it's Jibril." This is a huge joke. So I laugh. My laugh sounds strained and hysterical to me.

"Just put it down," he says, already bored by me.

I place the bagel beside his keyboard. "Capp?"

"Yeah, put it—"

I don't even have to pretend to spill the coffee. It happens. Yes, I planned it, but now it just happens.

"Aaahh aahhh!"

Coffee on his lap, his leg, his arm. Tommy pushes back violently, which dumps the last two inches of coffee on top of the rest.

"Idiot!" he shrieks.

He's up, backpedaling, patting at his clothes, and I'm saying "sorry, sorry, sorry," and snatching at napkins. He pushes me back, furious, and curses impressively.

Will he?

"Dammit, I have to go change."

Will he?

Yes. He runs off, muttering, and leaves his workstation on. As soon as he's out of view, I'm in. I'm shaking. I've hacked the systems at Spiker for years, but this is an individual workstation. This is the stuff too personal or too secret to put on the main servers.

I punch in the Adam code.

And just like that, I'm in.

The hard part is transferring the data. There's no USB drive. Is there Wi-Fi? There isn't supposed to be; there's no Wi-Fi at Spiker for security reasons. But ah, yes, the capability is still there.

I open Tommy's Wi-Fi, scan for the only active beacon. It's titled snakep. As in Snake Plissken, my more-or-less namesake from that movie *Escape from New York*. The only other Plissken I relate to.

File after file is now streaming to my phone. How much time do I have? I glance guiltily over my shoulder. With one hand I mop at the spilled coffee on the chair, just in case anyone is looking.

But my other hand pounds keys—I have a heavy touch—searching for whatever it is that Tommy is hiding. He's arrogant, fortunately, sure that no one can hack his computer, so the individual files are not password-protected.

There's a large file of photos. Probably porn or something. I open it, anyway—it might be useful to know Tommy's kinks.

But if these are someone's idea of porn, they have very, very strange tastes indeed.

I open more pictures.

I've stopped breathing.

I'm seeing long rows of Plexiglas tanks. Some are vertical cylinders. Some are horizontal rectangles.

Each contains a horror.

A full-grown pig with faintly green skin.

A hairless puppy with what looks like two human ears growing just behind its own ears.

A girl, a human girl, at least something like a human girl, but with two faces—one where it ought to be, and one stretched flat across her back.

"Oh God," I say out loud. I can't help it.

I shut the file. I swallow back the sour taste in my mouth.

Oh my God.

I hear a sound. Tap, tap, and I'm back in the fantasy football app as Tattooed Tommy returns, wearing the gym clothes he must keep for trips to the Spiker fitness center.

"Get the hell off my computer!" he snarls.

"I was just cleaning up the coffee that—"

"And spying on my picks!" His eyes narrow dangerously. "Did Wilma Petrov put you up to it? That bitch has been trying to figure out my lineup so she can . . . I'll kill her!"

"No," I say, doing my best to seem as if I'm lying poorly.

"Wilma!" he yells across the room. "Dirty pool, Wilma!"

I'm backing away, and I realize suddenly that I've left his Wi-Fi turned on. If he notices—

Tommy grabs me, not too gently, either. "Listen, kid: Next time Wilma bribes you, come see me. I'll double whatever she paid if you get her picks before Friday. Hear me?"

"Yes, sir."

I'm out of there. And now I just have to decide what to do with a secret that is so very much bigger than I had ever imagined.

I need to clean up the video record of me at Tommy's computer. I need to get all this stolen data safely stored on something other than my phone, which might be searched at any moment.

Then, after I put together the presentation that will, I hope, bring Terra Spiker down, I need to get it to Eve.

I need her to understand why I have to do this.

23

EVƎ

THE NEXT MORNING, MADDOX HAS HIS MONEY. I HAVE EXTRACTED MY OWN concession from Aislin: She's staying with me until her parents get home. They e-mailed her to say they're extending their trip for a week (Aruba) and I want her in a safe place. Just to make sure Maddox isn't still being hunted.

She accepted with surprising ease. Is it possible the girl is learning from experience, finally? Is it possible she's realized how toxic her relationship with Maddox is?

Or is she feeling sorry for her pal, the mutant?

Either way. I'm good with either.

I don't know how my mother got the money to Maddox. I told her his name and she said that's all she would need. She has toadies who do nothing but run her errands and cater to her whims. Blue M&M's? No problem. Bikini wax? Time and place. Run 9K to an inept drug dealer? Gotcha covered.

At 6:30 A.M., Maddox texted Aislin with: *Got it. Yur the best.*

I contacted the assistant principal at school to let him know Aislin had been in a minor accident. Some stitches, no big deal. I'm not sure he believed me, but this close to the end of school, the staff gets pretty laissez-faire unless there's a felony involved.

Also, they just rebuilt the gym with a giant check from my mother.

Dr. Anderson and his staff have chosen not to comment on my bandage-free leg and arm. Yesterday evening, when my mother arranged to have Aislin and me moved to one of the guest suites, Dr. Anderson even helped carry over my vases full of drooping flowers.

He looked a little bereft. I think he kind of liked having an actual patient. Especially one he knew he could cure.

"Where's Scruffy McMuscles?" Aislin asks, as we settle into my workstation. "You said he's working the coffee cart, right? I could use some caffeine. Or some other kind of stimulation." She attempts a leer, but it clearly hurts too much to pull off.

"I haven't seen him."

"Then I guess we'll have to make do with Adam." Aislin scratches her nose. "These stitches are driving me nuts."

"Yeah, I know how that goes."

"How would you know, Bionic Woman?" Aislin asks.

She's teasing, but I give her a sharp look.

"Too soon? Sorry." She pats my shoulder. "Back to work. Let's finish my fantasy man."

Adam is now a handsome head full of dark hair that floats in the simulated liquid of his environment.

It turns out the software has an interesting feature I hadn't noticed before. Not only can you age your creation up or down, you can adjust for lifestyle.

For the next hour, Aislin and I play with shoulders, chest, belly. We use slide bars to show the effects of our random choices. More or less appetite? More or less exercise? It's a useful lesson in the limits of genetics.

Adam has the genes for a ripped chest and six-pack abs. But if we give him too much of a sweet tooth and too little restless energy, his stomach balloons.

"Let's see what happens if he totally lets himself go," I suggest.

I slide a bar, and suddenly Adam has man boobs.

"His are bigger than yours!" Aislin squeals.

I slide the bar back. Quickly.

I make a mental note: When I'm putting finishing tweaks on his brain, I need to remember that a little hyperactivity might not be a bad thing. Maybe some bundle of genes that will make him crave the outdoors.

He needs to mountain bike. Play tennis. Something aerobic.

Maybe he could be a runner, like I am.

Aislin ogles Adam as he floats in midair like a ghostly Adonis. In the corner of the room, two secretaries whisper and giggle. Someone provides a wolf whistle.

"I think it's time to face facts," Aislin says. "Boy parts are on the menu."

"We haven't done the legs yet."

"Oh, I get it. We're going to kind of close in. Come at it from all other directions first. Leave the best for last." She elbows me. "Sort of the story of your love life, isn't it? Leaving the best for last. Or at least for much later."

"There's no rush to—"

"Or even much, much later, poor baby."

"Legs!" I yell the word. I don't mean to yell the word. I just do.

"Fine, legs," Aislin concedes. "Short and stumpy?"

"No," I say. "Although we can try them out. I mean, what am I doing here? Eliminating every imperfection?"

"Well, duh."

"But who's to say what's perfect?"

Aislin shrugs like it's a stupid question. Maybe it is. But I'd rather debate philosophical questions than sit here with my best friend and design things I've never actually, you know . . . seen. Except in diagrams in health class. And the occasional Google image by accident.

"Really, Aislin. Everybody's messed up in their own unique way, right? Nobody's perfect."

"Seriously?"

"Yes," I insist.

"Right. This from the girl who wouldn't let Finnian Lenzer ask her out because his hair was too blond?"

"He's practically an albino," I say. "Not that there's anything wrong with that."

"'Toine Talbert was too short. And John Hanover was too thin. And Lorenzo whose last name I forget had a funny face. And you blew off Carol because you're not a lesbian."

"That's not exactly my fault," I say.

"What did you expect Carol to think? You kept saying no to boys. Naturally she was going to think you played for her team."

"I'm not attracted to girls."

"But you are attracted to boys?"

"You know I am!"

"In theory. Not so much in reality."

"I'm selective."

"You said you couldn't go out with Tad. Why?"

I mumble something.

Aislin cups a hand to her ear. "What was that, now? You couldn't go out with Tad because . . . ?"

"Because his name is Tad!" I yell in frustration. "How can I date a guy named Tad? It's a ridiculous name."

"Also Chet."

"Chet? I'm going to date a guy named Chet? What is this, 1952? No one's named Chet."

"Mmm-hmm."

"I have legs to make," I say frostily.

"Make them short and bowed," Aislin says.

"You know I'm not going to do that."

"Oh, I know that," she says, triumphant. "You're going to make them long and muscular. You're going to slide the lifestyle bar all the way over to track star."

"Am not."

But of course in the end that's exactly what I do. Adam gets long legs. And muscular thighs. And well-developed calves.

He is now three disconnected bits. Leg. Leg. Torso and head.

There is, shall we say, a certain empty space in between those three pieces.

"The undiscovered country," Aislin intones in a video voice-over.

"Muffins, anyone?"

Solo enters, rolling the coffee cart.

"My point exactly," Aislin says, motioning him over.

I have several long, long seconds to wonder which is more embarrassing: a giant image of an Adam with a number of missing parts? Or an Adam with those parts?

"How're you feeling, Aislin?" Solo asks. He doesn't glance at me.

"I'm better now," she says, giving him an up-and-down. She grabs a cruller.

"Heard you moved out of the clinic," Solo says, looking at me for the first time.

"No point in staying," I reply flatly. "I'm a freak of nature, as you know."

"Yeah, well. I'm on food-cart duty for one more day," Solo says, as if I'd just told him I had a hangnail. "I thought I'd come by and see whether you need anything. Chips? Snickers bar?" He pauses, surveying our incomplete Adam. "Hot dog?"

Aislin leans forward, very serious. "Do you have anything heartier than a hot dog? Say, a kielbasa? Italian sausage? A whole salami?"

She is making hand gestures as she goes along.

Solo's face goes red. He's only good for about one round of flirtation with Aislin. After that he loses his way.

"He's shy," Aislin reports to me as if Solo isn't there. "I don't know: Should we make Adam shy? It's kind of cute."

"I'll take a sandwich. Not salami," I say. "Turkey."

Solo pulls a turkey sandwich off his cart. He hands it to me and snags a napkin. The napkin drops to the floor. I automatically reach for it, but Solo's already down on one knee. He grabs the napkin and hands it to me.

Except that when I reach for it, he's got my hand in his and the napkin is only part of what he's giving me.

Something small, maybe an inch long, hard and rectangular.

Our eyes meet.

He stands up.

"The other night, I noticed you had your laptop in your room," he says quietly. "MacBook Pro. A little old school, huh? Still has a USB drive."

And I know right then what he's slipped me. A thumb drive.

I can pull it out, notice it, hand it back to him. I can stop whatever he's up to right now.

I crumple the napkin in my lap in a way that Aislin won't see. I glance down and confirm that it's a flash drive. There's a small Apple logo.

Solo escapes from the room before I can say anything. Before Aislin can say anything else.

Aislin watches him go, enjoying the rear view with the practiced eye of experience. "If you don't, E.V., I just may."

I have a quavery, uneasy feeling in my chest. I don't know what's on that thumb drive. But I know it's a secret.

I know it's a secret from a boy who hates my mother.

Just a little longer and I can go home, I tell myself. I will have kept the deal with my mother.

And I'll be safe from Solo.

"I've got to pee," Aislin announces. "I'll be right back."

As soon as she's out of the room, I pull the flash drive from the napkin and examine it. Nothing special. And yet somehow, I'm afraid of it.

I wrap it up and shove it into my sweater pocket.

Adam hovers before me, glowing and gorgeous. My unfinished masterpiece.

Suddenly, I feel this explosive restlessness, a craving for the fog and steep streets of San Francisco. I want out of this place. I want to run until my brain shuts off, my legs scream with exhaustion.

Before I can lose my nerve, I cast a quick glance at the screen and randomly tap some options. I don't think about it; I just do it.

Aislin returns just as I hit the last button: *Apply Modifications.*

A hum, a flicker, and there he is. My perfect man, with nothing—and I do mean nothing—left to the imagination.

I tilt my head, squinting. "What do you think?"

Aislin executes a flawless wolf whistle. "Girl," she says, "I like your style."

24

I SLIP THE THUMB DRIVE INTO MY COMPUTER. THE ICON POPS UP ON MY desktop. Now all I need to do is click on it.

All I need to do.

It's late. Aislin is snoring softly. I faked sleep to get her to go to bed. I'm in the bathroom, in my pajama bottoms and T-shirt, sitting on the toilet with the seat down. The light is pretty awful for this time of the night. It's a no-secrets light.

The icon shows the Apple logo.

A click of the mouse or the touch of a finger on the screen is all it takes. Here's the thing, though: You can't un-know something once you know it. Once you know, you know. Once you know, you may be compelled to act. Once you act . . .

You're overthinking, I tell myself. Overworrying.

And yet . . .

Why is this so hard? Didn't I come in here for the purpose of seeing what is hidden within Solo's drive? Isn't that why I'm sitting on a hard toilet seat in the middle of the night?

I stick out my index finger, hovering over the screen.

Touch.

The file opens. It contains three other files. One is a video. The other two seem to contain documents or pictures. The video is labeled "#1."

I take a breath. I find my earbuds—they've fallen to the tile floor. I plug them in and stick them in my ears.

The video is of Solo. He's standing, kind of bouncing back and forth with energy. He's nervous.

"Eve. It' me, Solo."

I smile a little, in spite of myself. Like I wouldn't know that without him telling me.

"I don't know if you're going to watch this. I don't know what your reaction is going to be. You were never part of the plan. But . . . well, here you are. And I guess you're involved now. Now."

He seems to be losing his way. He starts to reach for the camera, as if he's going to turn it off. Changes his mind.

"Anyway, you're part of this because you are who you are. It's just that before, I didn't know you. I mean, I knew you existed. I knew about you, but then you became a real person. A person I liked."

He looks down at his feet. "A person I like a lot." Pause. Shuffle. "A lot."

I glance nervously toward the locked door, as if someone might overhear. But I'm the only one hearing. The only one feeling.

"So, anyway, you're Spiker as much as she is, I guess. So I'm laying this out for you." Long pause. I sense he's arguing with himself, regretting this. "I feel like you deserve to know every-thing."

Solo clears his throat. He reaches toward the camera and the video ends.

I'm in this deep. I click on the first file.

There are a dozen individual documents in the file. The first ones I open look like budget spreadsheets.

I don't really have any interest in budgets and I don't really know how to read a spreadsheet. Maybe they're incredibly mean-ingful, but I'm not the person to figure that out.

I'm disappointed.

But I keep looking. The next thing I open is a description of Project 88715.

PROJECT 88715, PHASE ONE: WE WILL UNIFY SEVERAL NEW AND MATURING TECHNOLOGIES DEVELOPED WITHIN SPIKER AND OTHERS FROM OUTSIDE THE COMPANY. THE GOAL WILL BE TO DEVISE A SIMPLIFIED USER INTERFACE THAT REDUCES THE EXTREME COMPLEXITY OF GENETIC ENGINEERING TO SUCH A LEVEL THAT ANY MODERATELY BRIGHT OPERATOR CAN CONSTRUCT A FULLY DEVELOPED HUMAN.

PROJECT 88715, PHASE TWO: WE WILL LINK THE USER INTERFACE PERFECTED ABOVE TO BEGIN ENGINEERING HUMANS.

I stare at the page. This is about the program I've been using, the one I am using to create Adam.

A program to allow the creation of simulated humans.

Except for one thing: It doesn't say anything about "simulated."

I open the remaining file. The pictures come spilling out.

There's a picture of a pig. Its flesh is green.

There's a picture of a puppy with ears, human ears.

There's a picture of a man with vacant eyes and folds of skin hanging from his chest like sails made of flesh.

There's, oh God, there's a girl with a face on . . .

There's a row of giant tubes, each with some living thing.

There's . . .

I'm sick to my stomach.

The pictures are still spilling out.

A cow that's all out of proportion, with an udder so large the legs couldn't reach the ground, even if she were on the ground and not floating in some kind of tank.

And then another giant tank, with something—someone?—suspended in it. I see hair, dark hair, swirling like seaweed, a hand, a foot, but that's all I can make out, because there's someone standing outside the tank, grinning. It's the scientist with all the tattoos.

The computer clatters from my lap.

I twist around, fall to my knees, and get the lid up before I vomit up what little is in my twisting stomach.

Dry heaves. Can't stop.

Oh, no, no, no. My mother . . . Oh God.

Aislin bangs on the door. "Hey, what's going on with you in there? Are you all right?"

I can't stop the heaves.

Aislin picks the lock. It's not hard. She has to step over me to get all the way inside. She places a calming hand on the back of my neck. Aislin has long experience with puking.

"Try to breathe, but only through your nose," she says helpfully.

She sits on the edge of the tub, prepared to wait it out. I hear her pick up my computer.

I try to say "no," but I can't find any words.

"Don't fight it, just relax into it," Aislin advises. "It's . . ." She falls silent. She's seeing.

"Oh my God," she says. "Oh, no. What is this? Oh . . . Oh no. No. No."

But of course, no is not the answer.

— 25 —

SOLO

I'M AWAKE WHEN SOMEONE POUNDS ON MY DOOR. IT'S NOT LIKE SLEEP IS AN
option. I'm so hyped up I can't lie still for long.

And if I close my eyes, even for a second, the horrifying
images from Tommy's computer are waiting for me.

The pounding intensifies. I throw on a pair of boxers.

For a moment, I wonder if it's Eve. She's probably viewed
what's on the flash drive by now—assuming, that is, she has any
intention of looking at it at all. Could be she just tossed it in the
nearest trash can.

I wonder, again, if I was wrong to share what I've learned.

No. Eve's like me. She'll want to know.

"Open the damn door."

A jolt of pure adrenaline shocks me into full alert mode.

It's Tommy.

He knows.

I have no choice. There's nowhere to run, not from here, not now. I unlock the door.

Two security guys burst in. One is older, graying. The other's young. He works out, I've seen him at the gym.

And then he appears. Tommy.

He reeks of sweat and dope. Beneath a skull tattoo on his neck, a blue vein throbs.

"Got into my files, didn't you? Clever boy. Dumped coffee on me. Jumped on my computer and used the old Wi-Fi. Smart boy. But were you smart enough to load it to the cloud? Or is it still trapped inside your computer?"

I don't answer.

Tommy strides over to the desk where my laptop and my pad both lie. He drops into the chair and taps the pad. The four-digit-code screen pops up.

"What's the password?"

"One, two, three, four," I say. I'm pleased at how calm I sound.

Tommy's skeptical, but he types it in, anyway. He scowls at me. "Cute. You have a separate security software installed."

I shrug. "Too easy to break a four-digit numeric password. So I added a little something."

"Give me the code."

I shake my head.

"You know, bagel boy, it's bad enough you left the Wi-Fi on," Tommy says. "You also neglected to consider the fact that I have three separate micro surveillance cameras installed at my work-station." He clucks his tongue. "Very sloppy."

"What can I say? I'm an amateur."

"Give me the code," Tommy snaps. He casts a significant look at one of the security guards.

A split second later my head's jolted by a full-palm slap.

It stings. But I box. I've taken a lot worse.

"Okay," I say. "Don't hurt me. The code is FG6H8D55lMSU1L-QWVFOP7FD34MHUTDLK."

Tommy types as I speak. "What is that, like, thirty charac-ters?"

"Thirty-two."

"Paranoid much?"

On the pad's screen, a graphic of a middle finger appears.

Tommy curses. He knows what I've done.

The screen goes dark. All the data on the pad has just been erased and rewritten. A lab with the right equipment and trained personnel might still be able to salvage some of it, but it would take days, maybe weeks. Even then they'd just get fragments.

"Want the password for my laptop, too?" I ask.

Tommy leaps up out of the chair. He still has my pad in his hand. He smacks it against the side of my head, shattering the glass.

He brings it down again, this time on the top of my head, hard, with both hands and all the leverage he can get.

I'm not exactly home for a few seconds. Not all the way un-conscious, but not functioning, either.

One of the guards, the younger one, pulls Tommy back before he can do me serious damage.

"Hey, hey, hey, Dr. Holyfield," the guard says.

I've never seen Tommy this enraged. I'm not surprised. But it's weirdly fascinating to see such an intelligent man so lost in fury. He's spitting at me. He's cursing. He's straining against the guard until the tattoos on his arms are stretched and distorted.

It takes surprisingly long for him to get hold of himself. Eventually, the guard lets him go. Tommy paces, fingers twitching. He shakes himself out, adjusts his shirt.

"Okay. Okay," he mutters, and I'm thinking he's calmed down, but just then he darts in and punches me, a good, solid left jab. Blood explodes from my nose.

The guards are worried. They step in to stop him, but he backs away, hands up. "He had that coming. Little punk."

Blood runs from my nose and more streams of it come rolling down from my head, pooling in my eyes. I'm still trying to get my scattered wits back.

"Who have you talked to about this?" Tommy asks.

I make a mistake. I say, "No one." But I say it too fast, and he picks up on it.

"No one, huh? What's 'no one's' name, huh?"

He looms over me and I don't think the guards will be enough to stop him if he decides to nail me again.

"You guys are going to be dragged into something very heavy," I say to the security guys. "I don't think you're getting paid enough to be involved in major felonies."

They exchange a glance. I've hit home.

"Walk away right now," I tell them. "You haven't done that much so far. We can let—"

Wham!

Tommy nails me again and this one really hurts.

"Whoa," he says, examining his effort. "That's going to be ugly tomorrow. Of course"—he moves in close—"a couple days from now, you'll be good as new, won't you?"

"Dr. Holyfield, you gotta chill, man, he's right," the younger security guard says.

"It's all recorded, geniuses," Tommy says. "We already have video of you two. And about the only person who can make that go away is me. So you are already deep in it. But bagel boy makes a good point: You aren't being paid well enough. Which is why I'm going to give you each, what, let's say five grand?"

"Each," the older guard growls.

Tommy grins at me. He reaches out one finger and swipes the blood from my forehead. He sticks the finger in his mouth and licks it.

"Deal," Tommy says.

And it's that easy. My life has been bought for ten thousand dollars.

26

EVƎ

THERE'S A BELL AND A BUTTON. I STARE AT THEM FOR A WHILE.

It's late. And I don't want Solo getting the wrong idea. Me coming to his room. Wearing . . . what am I wearing? Belatedly I look down and consider the matter.

The gym shorts I sleep in. And the T-shirt. And the lack of bra I also sleep in. And a pair of untied sneakers I slipped into on my way out.

I should have brought Aislin. She volunteered.

But, I don't know, it just felt wrong. This is about my mother, which means it's about me. And Solo.

I'm shivering, and it's not because of what I'm wearing.

I push the buzzer.

He doesn't answer. I buzz again. Nothing. I press the buzzer and hold it down. I don't care if he's asleep, he can damn well wake up and let me in.

The door flies open.

A man—no, more than one man—rushes out. One of them slams me against the wall. I trip and slip to the ground. A third man stampedes by with a heavy step on my once-severed leg.

The door to Solo's room is ajar. Something is wrong, terribly wrong. Solo isn't one of the three men.

I climb up and rush into the room. Stupid, really, I probably should call for help or something. I think of this too late.

Solo is in a chair.

The first thing I notice is the blood.

The second thing I notice is the ropes.

"Close the door," he says in a clotted voice. "Dead-bolt it."

I do it. Then I rush to him, kneeling down so I can look up into his face.

"Gruesome, huh?" he asks.

He's wearing nothing but boxers. Thin rivulets of blood have made it all the way down to his shoulders and onto his chest.

"I'll get help," I say. But I know that's the wrong answer.

"No. There's no help in this place. They're just shook up because they didn't expect you." Solo works his tongue around his mouth. He grunts, and a second later spits out a tooth. "Sorry."

I run to his bathroom, soak a hand towel in ice-cold water, and run back. Carefully I blot the blood from his head. It's shockingly red on the white towel. I can't do a very thorough job because his hair is thick.

I wipe the blood from his face. Forehead. Eyes. Mouth.

I go back to rinse the blood out and as the cold water runs, my brain is racing, then stalling, then racing again, like a very bad driver with a very fast car.

I bring the now-pink towel back and begin to wipe the blood from his neck and chest.

I expect more blood to flow—they say head wounds bleed a lot—but it's barely a trickle.

I wipe down to the waistband of his boxers.

I look up at him and I'm a little startled. I'm disturbed in about six different ways. I haven't seen this much blood since it was coming out of me on Powell Street.

I haven't ever been knocked down, pushed aside before.

I've never touched a boy's body before.

I've never knelt in front of a boy before, a boy wearing nothing but boxers and rope.

Rope? "You're still tied up!"

"Yeah, I noticed that."

I jump to my feet, flustered and scared and overwhelmed. My fingers pick weakly at the knots.

"There's a Swiss Army knife in my dresser drawer."

I find it beneath rolled socks. Carefully, carefully, because I don't trust my trembling hands, I cut him loose.

He stands, turns, faces me, and says, "You looked at the files."

But I don't want to talk about it. Because all of that is so horrible and so complicated, and right now he is just so close.

"You—" Solo begins.

He stops talking, too.

We are inches away from each other. If I lean forward, my nose will touch the hollow of his neck.

Somehow we are closer now.

He breathes out and I breathe in.

Closer. My breasts touch the top of his abdomen. A shudder goes through him.

Through me, too.

His fingers tremble as they touch my cheek. I swallow hard. There's blood on his fingers, and now there's some on the back of my neck because his hand is under my hair and we are no longer inches away, we've gone metric, we are millimeters away and he breathes and I breathe and we both make shaky sounds like we might both be dying but not yet.

Nothing has ever moved as slowly as his mouth coming down toward mine.

It's a million years.

His lips touch mine.

So, some part of my brain thinks happily: That's a kiss.

Oh yes, that is definitely a kiss.

Some years and decades and eons later we pull apart. And he says, "Now: We have to run."

27

WE RACE TO MY ROOM AND ARRIVE PANTING, THE TWO OF US BABBLING TO Aislin about beat-downs and crazy people and cover-ups.

"We have to get out of here!" I conclude.

Aislin cocks her head. "You have blood on your mouth."

"What?" I can feel the furious blush. "I must have cut my lip."

"Yeah. It's not *your* blood, honey," she says. She turns to Solo. "So, I guess I missed my chance with you?"

"Um . . ."

"Where are we running to?" Aislin asks. Not upset, mind you, just curious. As though fleeing from my own mother and her crazed minions is a perfectly normal, everyday occurrence.

"Just out of here," Solo says. He touches the cut on his scalp and grimaces. "Do you still have the flash drive?"

I dig in my purse and produce the little device with the Apple logo.

The three of us look at it, sitting in my palm.

So small, so dangerous, so terrible.

"Good." Solo nods tersely. "Hang on to it."

I rush to pull on jeans, turning away to put on a bra and T-shirt. Only then do I realize that I'm facing a mirror.

"He didn't look," Aislin says. In a mystified voice she adds: "He really didn't."

"I have excellent peripheral vision," Solo says, winking a blood-caked eye at Aislin.

"What about Adam?" I say. The thought has come out of nowhere.

"What do you mean, what about Adam?" Aislin asks. "We're fleeing for our very lives and you're worried about some software?"

"It's just—" I begin. But that's all I have.

Solo says, "Tommy didn't get his PhD and this job by being an idiot. We surprised him. We threw him off his game. But he'll be back. We have minutes—if that."

"My mother won't hurt me," I say, sounding pretty doubtful even to myself.

"But what about Solo?" Aislin says. "He's not her son." A strange look crosses her face. "You're not, are you?"

"No, thank God," he says with an ugly snarl. Belatedly, he realizes how that will sound to me. "I mean—"

I wave him off. "Let's get out of here," I say, but for some reason, I stop long enough to grab my sketchbook. I rip out my unfinished life drawing, fold it up, and stash it in the pocket of my jeans.

The three of us race out into the hallway. It's all very action movie, but feels ridiculous. Seriously, I'm fleeing from my mother? Seriously?

My mother, who made me a lab rat. My mother, who runs a chamber of horrors.

Those images. So many of them. How am I supposed to reconcile them with my mother?

The problem is, it's all too easy. It's not like she has ever been some warm, nurturing, hugging, head-patting type. She's an amoral bitch. That's the reality.

I'm running down curving, carpeted hallways, trying to dredge up something nice to think about my mother.

It suddenly occurs to me—and yes, it's a ludicrous setting and circumstance—that I've been a bit neglected as a daughter.

We make our way toward the garage, just like we had in our earlier "escape." But the risks are higher this time. The sense of fun is gone.

We climb into the elevator. It moves, comes to a stop.

The door doesn't open.

Solo nods, unsurprised. "He's after us." He pulls out his phone. "This will work once. Only once. He'll counter immediately."

He punches numbers into the keypad.

"We're between four and five. He's going to have the garage covered, and if he corners us down there, it's way too easy for him to finish us off."

The elevator lurches. "We're going back up," Aislin says.

"Yes," Solo says tersely. "Soon as the door opens we run."

"Where?" I ask.

"Just stay with me."

The elevator comes to a stop and we explode out the door. Solo yells, "This way, this way!"

We dash fifty feet down a long hallway. Solo stops at an office, panting, and stabs some numbers into a keyboard. The door opens. It's dark inside.

"Office belongs to a dude who's been on medical leave for months," Solo explains.

Aislin reaches for the light switch.

"No." Solo shakes his head. "No lights."

There isn't much to see in the office except the view out over the San Francisco Bay. Clouds hang thick on the Golden Gate. The stars are sparse, the moon visible only as a silvery glow without distinct location.

Solo pulls open a file drawer. "Either of you ever do any mountain climbing?" He has a big coil of rope in his hands.

"I have," Aislin says.

I blink at her, sure it's a joke. But she's taken a length of webbing and some metal rings from Solo. She weaves the webbing through her crotch, pulls out one loop of the webbing, and clips on the ring.

"What?" she says, in response to our shared amazement. "It's not all parties. My dad's taken me top-roping at Tahoe a few times."

We move out onto the balcony. The Spiker building glitters beneath us, spreading off to our right, a massive ornament of light perched above black water and invisible rocks. Solo ties the rope to the balcony railing and tosses the coil over the side.

He's chosen his location perfectly. It's one of the view spots in the complex where there's a clear drop without terraces in the way.

The coiled rope falls into darkness. Has it reached the ground? No way to know. I can only hope Solo has planned well.

"Okay, Aislin, you go first," Solo says. He helps her climb over the railing. "The figure eight may get twisted, so be careful."

To my amazement, Aislin understands what he's talking about.

She checks the rope and the carabiner like a pro and winks at me. I lean over to watch her fall, holding my breath. I'm not a big fan of heights.

She's sort of bouncing down the side of the building, feet hitting balcony rails and plate glass, pushing off, dropping another few feet.

She disappears from sight.

"Is she okay?" I ask.

Solo points to the knot. "The rope is slack. She's down, she's unhooked, and she's fine. Your turn."

"I don't know how to do that," I say. Now that I'm faced with actually climbing over the railing, leaning back with nothing but a rope, I'm having serious doubts about this plan.

"Listen, you just need to—"

"I'm not a wimp," I interrupt. "I could kick your ass in a 10K, no sweat."

"I have no doubt of that."

"But I don't, you know, like high places. Falling from them, anyway."

"I'll carry you down," Solo says.

"Not happening."

"We are short on time, Eve. Tommy is on the hunt. Like I said, he's not stupid. And if it hasn't happened already, your mother will have security all over this. We have seconds." He scrunches down a little so he can look me in the eye. "Don't worry. I won't drop you."

"I could beat you in a 5K, too," I add.

"Climb over the rail."

I do it, fast, before I lose my nerve. The wind is cold and strong. I'm extremely aware that if my feet slip I'll have a few seconds to scream before I hit the bottom.

I may be genetically modified, but I doubt my physical repair ability extends to recovering from death.

Solo swings easily over the railing. He loops the rope through his harness. He leans back, confident.

"Climb on," he says.

"How?"

"Your arms around my neck, your legs wrapped around my waist. Try not to choke me."

His body is at an angle to the building. He has one hand free. The other holds the trailing rope. Keeping all available hands on the railing, I turn to face him.

He pulls himself in closer, presses his body against mine.

Putting my arms around his neck is the easy part. The harder part is wrapping my legs around him. It feels ridiculous, and he has to lean slowly back to take my weight.

My calves are pressed hard against him. I don't know what to do with my head. So I just look at him, and he looks past me at the rope. "Eve?" he says. "You okay?"

"Why do you insist on calling me Eve?" I ask, because I don't really want to address the question of how okay I may or may not be.

"Dunno. Just feels right," Solo says, and then we start to fall.

We float downward. When we slow and gently bounce, it drives me against him. We drop again and bounce. Fall, slow, impact. Fall, slow, impact.

"See?" Solo says, pausing halfway down. "It's not hard."

It takes me a few beats to realize he's talking about the rappelling.

I snork a sudden, very stupid laugh.

He gets it, grins, looks away, and we bounce off again, falling, and now the truth is I am in no hurry to get to the bottom.

A final drop, and we land.

Aislin is waiting. It's dark, so I can't see her face very well, but her mocking, fake-disgruntled voice is clear enough.

"That's so unfair. No one even told me coming down that way was an option."

28

WE ARE IN WEEDS AND ROCKS BENEATH STUNTED TREES. THE GROUND IS SO STEEP no one has ever made much of an effort to landscape it. It's almost vertical from the foundation of the building down to the water.

"There's a staircase, if we can get there before it occurs to anyone to cut us off," Solo says. He points. "This way. Watch the branches—they might snap back as I push through."

It's not far, a hundred feet maybe, but it's a struggle to avoid losing our footing.

The stairs turn out to be wooden, a little ramshackle. They must have been here before the Spiker complex was built. It's dark, but there's some moonlight bouncing off the water, so while I can't see the steps, I can see the handrail.

Solo is in the lead, then Aislin, and I'm at the back. We try not to make noise, but the stairs creak and our breathing seems incredibly loud in the stillness.

"What do we do at the bottom?" I hiss.

"There's a boat," Solo calls back in a loud whisper.

It's ridiculous, but I was almost hoping we'd have to swim somewhere. I'm an excellent swimmer. I could easily make the team, but I don't want to be in cold water every morning before school. I'd like to show off my competence at something, after not exactly impressing during the rappelling event.

Then: "Someone's coming!" I say, loudly enough, maybe, for Solo and Aislin to hear.

Powerful flashlights stab cylinders of light into the darkness. There are three beams, then a fourth, and one is on me, lighting up my arm and the side of my face, blinding my right eye.

"There they are!" a man's voice cries.

They're at the top of the steps. They are not trying to be quiet. They are thundering down after us, their lights bobbing wildly.

The water is close. I see a wooden pier. I see two boats, both small, open motorboats. One has a wooden hull and the other is an inflatable Zodiac-style boat.

Two boats are worse than one. One boat is an escape. Two boats are a chase.

Solo leaps into the wooden boat.

"Cast off!" he yells to Aislin and me.

Aislin says, "What?" But I dive toward the stern rope. It's looped over a cleat. Aislin sees, understands, and starts to tug at the bow rope.

I hear the sound of a starter.

"Get them, get them, get them!" someone shouts.

A man, no two, hit the pier, two big, football-player-size guys charging at us.

Solo's hand flashes out and I am yanked bodily through the air, swung aboard. I hit my knees on the bench and trip. My hands plunge into the few inches of cold water in the bottom of the boat.

Aislin jumps and lands hard, but her impact pushes the boat a few inches from the pier.

The engine catches. There's a hoarse roar and the smell of diesel fuel.

The first of our pursuers leaps.

The boat is two feet away from the pier and gathering speed. The man misses, smacking his face against the side of the boat as he falls.

The other three men skid to a stop.

Solo grabs an orange life jacket and tosses it toward the churning water where the man has gone under. "Hey! Get your man or he's going to drown!" he yells.

The engine roars and we zoom away into the night.

"They'll lose a couple of minutes getting him out of the water, but they'll be after us soon," Solo says.

"Which boat is faster?" I ask.

"Excellent question," he allows. "I don't know."

Once again the fog—a regular feature of the bay—scuds across the moon. The milky light dies. We could run into a brick wall out here and not see it coming.

"What now?" Aislin asks, panting.

Solo's at the wheel. It's too low for him so he has to sort of squat. It's not a noble or attractive stance. His hair flutters in the breeze, except where some of it is matted with blood.

We are a sad, motley-looking crew. Aislin still sports a black eye and Solo . . . well, now that I look, his battered face is already looking better. But the boy needs a shower.

I glance over my shoulder at the towering mass of the Spiker building. Some offices are lit, some are dark. It's by far the brightest thing in view, and I'm strangely drawn back to it. It's dark everywhere else. Back there is dry and safe and well-stocked with food. Out here? Out here we don't even know what direction to steer.

"We can pull into Angel Island," Solo says loudly, trying to be heard over the noise of the motor. "There's no one there but some campers and a small caretaker staff. But we don't have sleeping bags or tents. Otherwise, we keep going to the city."

There are numerous cities in the Bay Area. But "the" city can only mean San Francisco. My hometown. I look for it, but it's completely hidden behind a wall of fog. Not a light showing.

I see flashlights all the way back on the pier.

"I have an idea," I say. "Do we have a flashlight?"

"Look in that locker," Solo says.

I rummage through fishing tackle, water bottles, and life vests until I find a flashlight. I test it within the concealment of the locker. It works. And it's a good, waterproof light.

I grab one of the life vests and wind a strap around the light. I make it as secure as I can.

Then I switch on the light and place the life vest over the side. It bobs away in our wake, then is caught by the current as the tide rushes out toward the Golden Gate.

"Smart," Solo comments.

"They'll see the light, figure it's us," I say. Then I add, "People will always go toward the light, won't they?"

No one answers. We all know it's not true: Sometimes people head straight for darkness.

"I don't like camping," I say. "Head for the city."

29

SOLO

"So," Aislin says after we've tied off the boat at Fisherman's Wharf. "Now what?"

"My plan never really went any further than this," I admit.

The wharf's asleep, but in a few hours the boats will start to come in. Then the early bird tourists will show up, looking for a latte and a croissant.

For now, it's a fog-wreathed ghost town of seafood restaurants and closed knickknack shops. The tour boats and ferries rock and creak at the piers. The stainless steel tables, which will soon be piled with crabs and fish on beds of crushed ice, are covered with canvas tarps.

A lone homeless guy pushes a heavy-laden Safeway cart, pauses to look into a trash can, and ignores us. A police car drives by and the fog swirls around the car. The cop ignores us, too.

Eve and Aislin look at me. I shrug. "Guys, I never planned to have two girls with me."

"Well, that's typical," Aislin drawls. "Men always want two girls, but do they take the time to plan? No."

"We need to get the data safely uploaded somehow," I say. "Once it's all over YouTube and Imgur.com, with links at Reddit, we'll be safe."

"Then what happens?" Eve asks.

I clear my throat, force myself to look her in the eyes. "Then the FBI and the FDA and a bunch of other agencies find out about it and move in."

"Move in." It's not a question, just a statement.

"We can go to my house," Aislin says doubtfully.

Eve shakes her head. "First place my mother will look."

"Where's the last place she'll look?" I ask.

Eve considers the question carefully. I see that she's thought of something. The idea makes her frown. She's not sure.

"I know a place," she says finally. "Follow me."

It's a bit of a walk along the Embarcadero, the boulevard that follows the waterfront around the northeastern tip of the peninsula. On our left are the massive pier warehouses. Many have been turned into tourist destinations. Some are more rough and ready. On our right are the streetcar tracks, and beyond them, almost wholly swallowed up by the fog, lie the hills and the tall buildings of San Francisco.

I can just make out the top third of Coit Tower, a concrete art deco structure, poking out of the fog. It was built with money left by a woman named Lillie Coit, a gambling, cigar-smoking, fire department groupie who shaved her head to pass as a man back in the twenties when that kind of thing would get you in trouble—even in San Francisco. I've always liked her story.

I like rebels.

We turn off the Embarcadero, heading down the side of the least-rehabbed warehouse. It extends out over the water, a shambling, corrugated tin-walled bit of history. There's a small door at the end. Its padlock is crusted with spiderwebs and rust.

Eve stops. With a tentative finger, she touches the lock.

"I might be able to find something to break the lock," I say.

Eve doesn't answer. She takes a deep breath, goes to the railing over the water, and kneels, fumbling until she finds a length of rotting, seaweed-tangled rope. She pulls it up.

There's a bobbing float on the end, even slimier than the rope. The float has a screw-off top that Eve isn't quite strong enough to manage. It's all I can do to budge the top. It doesn't want to open up. But at last it gives and inside there's a key.

Eve tries it. It works. She pushes the door inward and Aislin and I step in after her, batting aside cobwebs.

Eve finds a switch. A single lightbulb high overhead barely touches the shadows. We're in a big, open space, but not an empty space. Huge shapes rear up over us like creatures frozen in time.

The lightbulb pops and goes out. We all jump.

Eve takes out her phone and uses the light from it to locate a long table. It's a workbench, really, just some plywood nailed together. She rummages in a drawer and pulls out a package, ripping it open with her teeth. I hear a muted crack.

It's a glow stick. Blue light. A second glows green.

The light isn't much better, but my eyes adjust and I see that shapes scattered through the room are abstract statues of some kind. There are forms from nature—trees, I think, flowers, even clouds—but most of the sculptures resemble animals. Next to me, rendered in smooth, white stone, is the suggestion of a ten-foot-tall bear. Near Eve I can make out a tiger in mid-leap—or maybe it's a lion. No, it definitely feels like a tiger to me.

There must be seven or eight of these strange animal shapes. None of them look precisely like anything, but they all manage to tell you what they might be, could be.

"I haven't been here in a long time. Not since he died," Eve says. She sits on the floor, browsing through a stack of canvases leaning against a wall like tumbled dominoes.

I'm about to ask who she means, but it's obvious Aislin knows. She puts her hand on Eve's arm and says, "I wish I'd known your dad."

"Your dad was a sculptor?" I ask.

"Yeah," Eve says, and even that single word comes out shaky with emotion. "He did some painting and drawing, too. But mostly he sculpted."

I find the package of glow sticks. I snap one—it's blue, too—and use it to explore the room. There is something moving about this place. Something sacred, somehow.

"Won't your mother know you'll come here?" I call back to

Eve from behind something that must be a hawk or an eagle. It's hanging from the rafters by chains, and it doesn't look happy about being chained.

"My mom doesn't remember he was ever alive," Eve says.

"How did he die?"

"Car accident in Tiburon. I was eleven."

My heart pulls a lurch. "Where?"

Tiburon.

Eve's seventeen.

I do the math.

She shrugs: It's an unimportant detail. "Paradise Road, the back road to Tiburon. It's a twisty, two-lane . . . well, you know that."

Yes. I know.

Pieces fall into place. Pieces I never suspected.

My history with Eve goes much further and deeper than I know.

So that's why Terra Spiker took me in: guilt.

Her husband killed my parents.

Six years ago on a foggy night, someone tried to pass my parents' car. The driver must have seen oncoming traffic, because he suddenly swerved back and hit my parents, knocking their car over the side of the embankment.

The two cars crashed down through trees and rock, spraying dirt in every direction, the passengers smashing again and again against the dashboards and the steering wheels and roofs until they were all dead.

At least, that's how I see it sometimes, in my nightmares.

There was no way to know if the guy trying to pass my parents was drunk. The vehicles caught fire and burned for hours before anyone noticed and called 911. They identified my parents from dental records.

Terra never said a word. No one did. Maybe I would have pieced things together, if I'd read the accident reports, done some digging.

But I didn't want to know anything. One moment, my parents were alive. The next, they were gone.

I shut down. Shut off the world.

"That's a dangerous road," I say.

Then I find some other part of the room to be in.

• • •

I PACE BY ONE OF THE GRIMY WINDOWS, THINKING THINGS THROUGH. ALL I HAVE to do is make everything on the flash drive public. Once that's done, we're home safe.

Just one problem: We're stuck in a big warehouse full of massive statues and no Wi-Fi. There's no Internet of any kind.

Our phones all have connections, of course, but I have no way to get the files from the flash drive to the phone. I need a computer. A somewhat old-fashioned one, in fact, so that I can plug into a USB, then upload the files.

Damn.

I'm going to need a public library or a FedEx office or something. But it's 4:30 in the morning.

Nothing to do but sleep.

I'm weary. The adrenaline's worn off. I still feel bruised and battered, although I'm much better off than I should be. Poor Aislin's probably still feeling a lot worse.

"I guess we should try to sleep," I say.

There's a sagging couch, a cot, and a chair in one corner. A TV, too. I switch it on, but while someone is paying the electricity bill, no one has paid cable. I fiddle around a bit and get the local broadcast channels. There's nothing on, but the cold light is comforting, somehow.

"I've got the chair," Aislin says. "And I also have the couch. You two will have to share the cot. Oh, and I'm a very heavy sleeper. You guys could make all kinds of noise and I wouldn't even notice."

"Cute," Eve says. "I'll take the chair. I'm the smallest."

I stretch out on the couch. A couple of hours ago I was kissing Eve. I was sure I was madly in love with her.

I *am* madly in love with her.

But. But something's changed. I'm here in the studio of the man who killed my parents. Eve's father. Terra Spiker's husband.

Terra, who's done horrible things. To Eve, to me, to a whole lot of others.

There's too much history. There are way too many complications.

What did I think was going to happen after I revealed the truth? This isn't exactly a happily-ever-after kind of setup.

"I can't sleep," Eve says softly. I'm not sure if she's talking to Aislin or to me. To anyone. "I keep seeing . . . the girl."

No one asks who she means. We know.

"I wish you'd never shown me," Eve says, and now I'm sure she's talking to me.

I sit up on my elbows. "So you could live in blissful ignorance?" I ask. "I did you a favor, Eve."

"A favor?"

"She's your mother. You have a right to know. An obligation."

"Just because I'm her daughter doesn't make me responsible for what she's done," Eve says. "Are you responsible for your parents?"

I let it sit, and a moment later I hear her sharp intake of breath. "Oh, God, I'm sorry, Solo. I forgot. I'm so tired, I don't know what I'm saying anymore."

"Don't worry about it."

"It's just, she's my mother. You think you know someone, know what someone's capable of, and then—"

"Yeah, life's full of surprises," I say. I lie back, exhale loudly.

Then I rest the crook of my elbow on my eyes and pretend to fall asleep.

30

ADAM

I OPEN MY EYES.

I see something. It's a picture. It's a picture I know. It was already in my brain before I ever saw it. Now the sight of that picture resonates.

It's a girl.

The picture slowly cross-fades to a different picture. Same girl. This time she's at poolside with another girl.

This picture in turn cross-fades to the original girl, and her name pops into my head.

Evening. Her name is Evening.

I'm sitting upright in a chair.

I'm staring at a monitor.

Why? When did I move to this chair? How did I get here? Where was I before?

I reach a tentative hand to my head. There's a tight band, and I can feel wires, dozens of them trailing out and away.

Is this normal? I have thousands of images of people. None of them have a band with wires.

Yet another picture of Evening.

I love Evening.

How do I know that? It's obvious. It's true. I have to love her. She made me. I have the pictures in my head, moving and still, of Evening at a console making the decisions that would soon define me.

I see myself through her eyes, unformed, partial, incomplete. I see that she chose my hair and my face. I know that she sculpted my chest. That she had the vision to create perfect, muscular legs.

I am perfect. I'm Adam.

Perfect for Evening.

Mine is the face she will find impossible to resist. Mine is the skin she will long to touch. As I will long for hers.

She designed my body. She wants me to be her mate. Of course she does.

I haven't been told this, but I know it. I can draw my own conclusions.

In fact, I realize, I haven't been told anything. No one has spoken to me. I just . . . arrived . . . here in this chair. Came here from nowhere and nowhen.

I am wearing clothing, so I can't see my perfect, Evening-sculpted legs or my artfully symmetrical biceps or my hard abdomen.

"How did I come here?" I ask.

It's the first time I have spoken. I search my memory. Can it be true? Surely I have spoken before. To someone. But my memory reveals no someone.

I've just been born. The realization shocks me. I've just been born. But my memory tells me that is not the way it happens. My memory tells me of wombs and mothers and wrinkly, squalling infants.

None of that applies to me. I am full-grown. I am not a weak, dependent baby; I am strong and tall and I love Evening.

"You have always been here," a voice says.

A woman steps into view. She's tall, beautiful, glittery.

"There is no always," I say. "Nothing persists forever."

"Nothingness persists," she says. She is testing me.

"No. So long as anything exists, nothingness is impossible. In fact, it's nothingness that cannot persist. Nothingness gives way to somethingness. The nothingness that preceded the Big Bang was obliterated. Nothing became something."

The woman nods. "Good. You've absorbed data well. Your intelligence is obviously fully functional. You sound like a college freshman taking his first philosophy class way too seriously, but that's good. Evening will like it."

"I would still like to know how I came to be," I say.

"Consider it a mystery," Terra Spiker says. "Like the Big Bang. One second there's nothing, and the next second there's a universe."

"Evening created me."

"Yes, she did. And now you're going to find her. You're going to bring her here. For you, she'll come back."

"Where is she?"

Terra Spiker says nothing for a long time. I wonder if she hasn't heard me. But I can see that she is thinking. Her forehead creases. Her eyes narrow.

She corresponds to images I have of thoughtfulness.

"I have an idea where she might be," she says at last.

"What if she won't come with me?"

"Oh, she'll come," Terra Spiker says. "It's the fate of all creators: They fall in love with their creations."

31

EVƎ

It's a gray, halfhearted dawn, cold as hell, a fairly typical San Francisco morning, no matter the time of year. The fog isn't as thick
or as low as it was last night. It looks as if it might burn off later.

Solo will wake at any moment. And when he does he's going
to ask me for the flash drive, and we're going to find a place to
upload it.

The sequence of events that will follow is lurid, even in my
imagination. I see my mother with her manicured hands in chrome
handcuffs. I see federal agents swarming all over Spiker, demand-
ing passwords, hauling computers off to labs that can crack them
open and make them spill their secrets.

I see my mother in jail. An orange jumpsuit.

She hates the color orange.

I see her in court. She'll have great lawyers, of course. But
the damning evidence will come from her own daughter. At the

very least she'll have to sign some kind of a deal. She'll lose her business.

The horrors will end.

But so will the work on Level One. Projects that might bring relief to millions or save tens of thousands of lives. Some kid in Africa lives or dies because of what I decide.

This is too much to think about. I need to focus on what matters. I've been manipulated, used, a guinea pig. I'm a mod, in Solo's casual phrase. A genetic experiment.

To achieve this, terrible crimes were done and nightmarish horrors were created.

I close my eyes and see the monsters in their vats.

I blink them away, focusing my gaze on the stack of my dad's paintings piled haphazardly against the wall.

They're good, some of them, really good. Still lifes, landscapes, a few hastily sketched faces. Charcoal, mostly. Some watercolor. There's one of me as a baby, with chubby cheeks and a single tooth.

My hand freezes on the last canvas. It's my mother. The oil pastel my dad attempted, then abandoned.

It's been worked and reworked. I can feel him struggling with the gaze, the smile.

Smiling has never been my mother's strong suit.

Still, there's a soft vulnerability to the eyes. A gentle sweetness to the mouth. This drawing was done by someone who loved my mother deeply. Without reservation.

I think back to the endless fights and icy silences. Is it

possible, beneath all that high-octane drama, that they really loved each other? Did he see something in her that I can't see?

I take my own sketch out of my jeans pocket. It's smeared at the folds. I compare it to the portrait of my mother, studying the strokes and smudges, moving an imaginary pencil over my drawing.

"Whatcha doing?"

Aislin joins me. She's still a mess, but beautiful in her tough-but-not-really way. She squeezes herself against the cold and lays her head on my shoulder.

"Let's go outside," I suggest in a whisper. "Don't want to wake Solo."

She grins. "Are you sure?"

The breeze is brisk and smells of fish. I look down at the water. There's a sea lion gazing back up at us hopefully. No doubt it expects breakfast. I'm not sure the sea lions in the bay ever actually fish anymore. I think they just wait for bits of burger and chalupa ends.

"I got nothing," I say. I display my empty hands. The sea lion dives smoothly and disappears.

"You should sleep," I tell Aislin.

"Mmm. Should. I don't really do 'should' all that well."

I smile. "I've noticed."

"You do 'should.'"

"Do I?" It's a genuine question. I'm not sure I know the answer.

"That was some scary stuff. On the computer," Aislin says. She sounds tentative. She's feeling me out.

"Yeah. Stuff from a horror movie."

"What are you going to do?"

I heave a big sigh. "I don't know yet. According to you I do the right thing. But what's the right thing?"

She laughs. "Really? You're asking me?"

I look at her. "You know, Aislin, I don't always agree with what you do. But you are a good person. All the way, deep down, you're a good person."

She squeezes my hand, but she doesn't believe me.

"Tell me, Aislin. What do I do?"

She heaves a sigh that's an echo of my own. "It's a hard thing to go against family," she says.

"My mother deserves it," I say. "If she's really responsible."

Aislin laughs a little bitterly. "Remember when my dad had that mistress, Lainey, and my mom kicked him out? For a while. Then she let him come back. And my mom's obviously got a drinking problem, but I think he still loves her. And despite everything I've done, they still haven't thrown me out."

"They don't even know where you are," I say. "Really, Aislin, are we using your family as some kind of example?"

It's harsh. It's thoughtless. I know it as soon as I say it.

"Actually, they do know where I am," Aislin says evenly. "Or at least where I was. I told them I was staying with you up in Tiburon. It's not my fault I'm not there anymore."

I absolutely should drop it. But I'm exhausted. I'm confused. I have all kinds of great excuses. "Gee, sorry my problems got in the way of my saving your butt."

Right there, I stick the knife in our friendship. The one thing I never wanted to be was the bitch of a rich girl.

I hate myself. It's immediate, I don't have to think about it, I hate myself. I want to cut my own tongue out. But it's too late.

There's a long silence. Aislin gives me time to take it back. But I don't. And I don't know why, except that I'm so hating myself I feel like I deserve her anger.

She heads inside. I stand, gripping the railing, thinking how unfair it is that I'm having to hate myself when I really just want to hate my mother.

The door opens again and Aislin comes back out, carrying her purse. She brushes by me.

I say . . . I say nothing. I'm that messed up. I say nothing.

It's some kind of overload. Too much of too much. I have the feeling I desperately need to cry. And I just don't have it in me to deal with another crisis.

I hear her shoes moving away down the pier. Then she's gone.

Self-pity rushes over me. Can't she see that I need her to stick with me? Doesn't she know what I've been through? I was nearly killed. I found out my mother's a criminal. I escaped with my life from some creep who works for my mom.

Or at least, Solo escaped. And took us with him.

Am I a hundred percent sure he's told me the truth? I don't even know him. One kiss—even that kiss—doesn't make us best friends forever.

No, bitch, your BFF just walked away.

Well, I'm sick of Aislin's neediness. And I'm suddenly wondering if I'm just being manipulated by Solo. After all, he's good with technology. Maybe all those pictures were a fake. Maybe this is all some elaborate fraud to let him hurt my mother. He hates her enough to do it.

Maybe I just need to grab a taxi and get back to Spiker and tell my mother . . .

No. No, I know that's bull. I healed in days from something that should have taken months. That much, at least, is true.

And my gut tells me those pictures were real.

They return to me, unwanted, like some hideous slide show. The pig. The girl. That tattooed freak, standing in the room of freaks.

The tattooed guy. It clicks: He's the same guy who came rushing from Solo's room.

Maybe he's the bad guy. Maybe he's guilty and my mother is innocent.

As bad as that is, it would be so much better than the alternative.

At least I owe her a chance to explain. Right?

I'm freezing. I'm going to get my phone and call her. I've turned off the tracking so she can't use it to find me. There's no risk.

I have to give her the chance. She may be a cold bitch, but she is, still, my mother.

And if she can't explain? Then I give Solo the flash drive.

Inside the warehouse it's not much warmer, but it's some improvement, at least. I go to my purse.

Solo is no longer on the couch. He must be . . . He must be where, exactly?

"Solo." Nothing. "Solo?"

I know then. I begin the careful, then increasingly desperate, search that will confirm what I already know: The flash drive is gone.

And so is Solo.

AƆAM

I AM FAMILIAR WITH THE FERRY, THOUGH I'VE NEVER BEEN HERE BEFORE. A driver has dropped me off at the pier. I have a wallet with money. I have a credit card, too. I have a phone that does everything. It even answers my questions.

I know each of these things, just as I know where to buy the ferry ticket, and how to go aboard. I know in advance what the terminal looks like on the other side of the bay—the bay that I also know even though I should not.

The ferry leaves from Tiburon, which is Spanish for "shark." I don't speak Spanish, but I know what that word means.

I'm a few minutes early. There's a coffee shop full of early morning commuters.

Do I like coffee? I don't know.

Terra Spiker says I absorbed well. My intelligence is functioning well. My body works. But no one has yet told me what I like or dislike. I only know that I love and care for Evening Spiker. She made me.

I walk into the coffee shop. I know how to order. It almost feels as if I have ordered before, but I haven't. It's puzzling.

I reach the counter. A woman is taking orders. Her eyes open wide. Her pupils dilate. She swallows hard.

"What would you like?" Her voice catches.

"Coffee. A cappuccino."

"Anything else? A pastry?"

"No. Not a pastry."

"That'll be three dollars and ten cents."

I count out some money.

I wait for my coffee. People stare at me. Some of the men don't like me. Some of the men do. All of the women like me. Some of them pretend not to notice me, but they steal a glance, then look away.

A couple joins the group of people waiting for their orders, a young man, maybe twenty, and a girl, maybe a little younger. The girl looks at me and her mouth opens. The boy moves between us, blocking the girl from view. She steps out from behind him. She's smiling just a little. She bites her lower lip.

My coffee is ready. I take it. I say, "Thank you."

"No, thank you," the barista says.

The ferry is pulling in. I can see it through the plate glass. I head toward it. A man holds the door open for me.

I'm aware that people are following me. They are not in a precise line behind me. They form a loose knot, keeping pace with me. They are close, but not too close. Other people are jostled. I am not.

The sun is coming up behind tree-covered Angel Island. The fog lies between us and the city and I know this because I know a great deal about the area, though I've never been here.

An idea occurs to me. I try to think of what lies to the east of this area. I make it as far as a city called Berkeley. I have detailed information that far, street by street information, but then the map in my head turns vague. I know that somewhere out there is a city called Chicago. And another one called New York. And a place called Europe. I know a little about them, but only a very little.

Interesting. I've been incompletely educated. I know a lot about finding Evening, and I know almost nothing about anything else.

I lean on the rail of the ferry, out on the bow where the salt spray flies up and soon moistens my face. A young woman comes to stand beside me.

"Excuse me, I know you must get this a lot, but are you a model?"

"No," I say. I'm curious. "Why would you think that?"

The young woman shakes her head ruefully. "You must know."

"I don't know a lot of things I should know."

"Dude, you are the most beautiful person I've ever seen."

"Am I?" I look around and see two girls nodding their heads in unison.

"Oh. Thank you," I say.

"You should definitely be a model. Or a movie star," the

young woman says. "Or do ads or endorsements or . . ." She shrugs.

"He could sell me anything," a middle-aged mom with two kids says. "Anything."

Their words make me uncomfortable. I hunch my shoulders forward and drop my head a little. Then I stare out at the water and refuse to look behind me until we are docked in San Francisco.

Terra Spiker has given me a list of three places to look for Evening. The first is the family home. It's a distance away in a neighborhood called Sea Cliff. I know that I can walk, or take a series of buses, or hail a cab.

There's only one cab and his "out of service" light is on. I will need to walk, or take the bus, unless—

The cab swerves across three lanes and the window goes down.

"You need a ride?" the driver asks.

EVƎ

I'M FRANTIC. I STILL HAVE MY PHONE, BUT I DON'T HAVE SOLO'S NUMBER.
I ask my phone where I can find a computer for rent. I follow the
directions and head toward it at a trot.

This is happening too fast. I can't let Solo do it.

Can I?

The copy center is closed. It doesn't open for another two
hours. I look around, desperate. I'm in the financial district now,
a midget at the feet of giants. The Transamerica Pyramid is in one
direction, the Bank of America building in the other. I head toward the B of A, hesitate, stop, wish I had psychic powers, look
carefully in every direction. Nothing. No one but a street person,
an older woman, who pushes a shopping cart toward me while
muttering, "I told her it was okay, I told her it was okay."

Schizophrenia, a genetic condition. The kind of terrifying disease that might be cured with the right knowledge, if you knew

just where to find the particular genetic codes and could snip, snip, paste, paste.

Would the mentally ill street person want to be cured if she knew that it meant a basement full of freaks and monsters?

Don't be a fool, I tell myself. Of course she would. Just about anyone would.

Where did Solo go?

He could be anywhere, I realize. He doesn't need to wait for some library or printing company to open. There are computers all around me. They're piled seventy stories high. Solo, being Solo, may have already found an office left unlocked, or charmed his way past a security guard. The odds are that the deadly data is already propagating across the Web.

This isn't his decision. It's our decision.

"Yeah, well, screw you, Solo," I say bitterly. "You can drop dead and die!"

I'm aware of the redundancy in that statement.

I head dejectedly back to the pier warehouse. I pause at a doughnut shop. I go in, telling myself I'll just grab a cup of coffee. I come out with a dozen doughnuts, some of them still so fresh they're hot. I devour two on my way home.

It isn't far back to the pier. The door's unlocked, just as I'd left it. Some part of me hopes Aislin's returned. I want to hear her tease me for resorting to comfort pastry.

Some other part of me is hoping Solo's returned, so I can scream at him and then, quite possibly, kiss him for several days.

More doughnut.

As soon as I'm inside, I know I'm not alone.

The rising sun beams through the high windows. It lights the tops of the statues glaring down at me with animal ferocity.

The sun also lights one side of his face.

He sees me.

He doesn't move.

"Evening?" he asks.

"Adam," I say.

– 34 –

SOLO

On the twenty-seventh floor of the Bank of America building I find a big law firm. They aren't open for business, but they work the lawyers hard at places like this. A rushing, harried young woman is on her way in. She fumbles with the key, gets it finally, and throws open the door before hurrying inside.

The door swings shut, but not fast enough. I stick the toe of my sneaker in, just barely, to keep it open. I wait three minutes to make sure the lawyer has gotten to her own office. Then I slip inside.

The lights are dim, the reception desk empty, the floors carpeted. I try to guess which way the lawyer has gone, decide it was to the left. I go right. Some individual offices are locked, others are wide open.

Their computers look pretty up-to-date, but I'm able to find one with a USB port. I enter the office and close the door behind me. There's a nice view down California Street.

The computer's password protected. I try the basics: 1,2,3,4. QWERTY. YTREWQ, which is querty backward. PASSWORD. A few others. Whoever uses this computer isn't quite that dumb. They are, however, dumb enough to write it down in the corner of the desk blotter.

I check the clock, stick in the flash drive. It's slow to load. Very slow, since there are a lot of hi-res images.

From here it will be simple. All I have to do is attach the file to a dozen e-mails: CNN, the *New York Times*, various members of Congress from both parties, contacts I know in the hacker collective Anonymous, the FBI.

I type the addresses in. Each will know the others have received the same documents, so there will be no chance of a cover-up.

All I have to do is push "send."

All. I have to do.

Is push "send."

What follows won't happen overnight. The world doesn't move that fast. But in days or weeks the FBI will descend on Terra Spiker.

Congress will schedule hearings.

Documents and files will be seized. In the end, likely, handcuffs will grind shut around the wrists of Terra and Tattooed Tommy and probably lots of others.

I sit, unmoving, staring at the screen.

A crime's been committed. Many crimes. Some may be more than criminal; they may be evil.

But I can't lie to myself and pretend that's my only motive. I'm angry at Terra Spiker for the life she's given me. For treating me like one of her low-level employees after my parents died. For keeping me, if not quite a prisoner, then close to it in the walled-off world of Spiker Biopharm.

For doing to me what she did to Eve.

"Do this," I tell myself.

Chaos and madness. Unleash it. What's that phrase?

Cry havoc?

I actually pause to Google it.

"Cry havoc and let slip the dogs of war," I read.

Then I read that "cry havoc" was a phrase from Shakespeare's day, a signal to soldiers to burn and pillage and rape.

So, a bad choice of things to think about.

Shakespeare used the phrase in two other plays. He must have liked it. One is something about a stained field. Bloodstains, of course. The third is from a play I've never heard of.

"Do not cry havoc, where you should but hunt with modest warrant," I read aloud.

I gaze at the words on the screen.

Seriously, Solo? You're hesitating? You've lived for this moment.

Let slip the dogs of war!

Or . . .

Hunt with modest warrant.

Just theoretically, I ask myself, what would that mean, to hunt with modest warrant? What's the step that isn't quite dogs of war?

I'm agitated. I feel bouncy and twitchy all of a sudden. Frustrated, in more than one way.

Really, Solo? A Google search stops you?

A Google search and a kiss. That's the truth of it. That's what has me jumpy and indecisive and looking for an excuse to just not go all dogs of war.

I'm a warrior. I *am* a dog of war. I've spent years . . . and now the will drains out of me because of a kiss and a Shakespeare quote?

Well, not *just* the kiss. The rope descent, that was . . . Yep, breathing a little harder at the memory, and whatever that brings to mind (I know exactly what it brings to mind). Whatever that memory means to me, if I drop my finger on that "send" key, a memory is all it will ever be.

The problem is that I can feel her legs wrapped around me, and I can taste her lips, and I can imagine, and imagination is a damned tease, imagination will torture you, but knowing that doesn't stop it. My imagination is off and running, running through places sweet and sweaty. And it's not just that, not just the sweaty parts or even the sweet parts, it's the feeling that my life is a laser beam that just encountered a mirror, that it's being bent, a sudden turn, a wild veer, a turn, all of that stuff, all that feeling that whatever the hell I thought my life was, maybe it's not. Maybe the whole story of Solo was just a way to get to this point, only the point is not the poisoned e-mail that rests half an inch below the index finger of my right hand, the point is something I never saw coming and surprise! the Solo story is not all what I thought it was.

Justice and revenge. Or Eve.

My hand flies back. As if I'd suddenly discovered the keyboard was a cherry-red stovetop.

I gasp.

I stare at my hand. My hand made the decision. My hand thinks I'm an idiot. My hand thinks only a damned fool would choose revenge over love.

I think my hand may be right.

One way or the other, the decision isn't mine to make alone. I need Eve.

EVƎ

"EVENING," HE SAYS AGAIN.

I nod. Too vigorously. Because my voice is sure to fail.

He's here.

But he can't be here.

He's real.

But he can't be real.

He's taller, somehow, in reality. His eyes are alive now, amazingly alive. He's curious, concerned. He knows me—that much I can tell. He knows who I am.

He's the most beautiful male I've ever seen. Ever. Anywhere. George Clooney and Johnny Depp and Justin Timberlake and all of them, all of them, would be cast as Adam's less attractive best friend.

I wonder, can he speak anything more than my name?

Although even that's great. I liked hearing him say my name. I'd like him to do it again.

"I've been looking for you," he says.

"Unh?" I respond brilliantly.

"Your mother sent me to find you."

It's obviously true, and the honesty of it surprises me. "Are you supposed to tell me that?"

"I don't know."

He doesn't shrug or smile or duck his head. I realize he has no affectations. He's acquired no little tics or habits.

The strangeness of seeing him leaves me speechless. He's a creature from a dream. He's something I doodled on a sketch pad, brought to life, fully formed.

I want to touch him. To ensure that he's real and not some weird trick of my tired mind.

I also just want to touch him. Because . . . just because.

And I believe I can touch him. I believe he will allow me. I believe this because he is, in some impossible way, mine. Does he know that?

"Do you know who I am?" I ask. I'm not just asking if he knows my name. I'm asking if he knows who I am, what I am. I'm asking if he knows my importance.

It's the kind of thing I've heard coming from my mother on more than one occasion: Do you know *who* I am? With italics on the "who" and a rising, incredulous tone on the "am."

I don't say it that way. But I mean it that way.

It's insane to even think like this, but despite the magnificence of this boy, he is in some sense mine. And I want him to know it.

You are mine, Adam.

Where the hell does that kind of thinking even come from?

"You are the one who designed me," Adam says. "I am your perfect match. Your soul mate."

"You know about all that?"

The first hesitation. He isn't being coy. He's considering. "I don't think I know all of anything, Evening."

I want to tell him to stop using my name because every time he does it sends a shiver through me. I don't want a shiver. I don't want him to make me weak in the knees.

I stay silent and he continues. "I have been given some information. It's a crude technique, I understand, so all I know is parts of things. I'm still being formed mentally. I have knowledge but no experience."

"That won't make you so different from most guys," I say. It's a smart-ass remark. A joke. Does he have a sense of humor? I gave him one. At least, I included the codes that would tend to allow him to develop a sense of humor, but does he have the experience to know a joke when he hears one?

"You made me different from most guys," he says.

That might be a semi-witty comeback. I'm prepared to accept it as such because I don't think I could ever have a relationship with a guy who has no sense of humor.

Relationship?

Back up there, girl.

Back right up against that . . . Okay, no. I'm now arguing with myself. Chiding myself. I'm in charge here, right? I shouldn't even be thinking about him as anything other than a very interesting experiment. He's my A-plus science project.

Some rational part of my brain points out that this—this person, this creation, whatever Adam is—is a walking crime. Real or unreal, living or fabricated, it doesn't matter. Adam shouldn't be here. Someone breathed life into him and sent him out into the world, and that was wrong.

But try as I might, I can't stand here two feet away from him and not react. I don't think there's a person of any gender, or no gender, for that matter, who could stand here and not react to him.

He is a work of art.

If I do say so myself.

"Okay," I say, mostly just to have something to say, because otherwise I'm just looking him up and down and up and down and it's impolite to stare. "What did my mother tell you to do once you found me?"

"She wants me to ask you to come back."

"That's it? No excuses or explanations? Just 'come back'? She didn't say anything else?"

"She said some things which I don't believe she wanted me to say to you. They were more in the nature of observations."

Poor guy, he seems to think I'd leave that alone. "Observations?"

"Statements."

I tilt my head quizzically. He starts to do the same, then stops himself. I inhibited his willingness to be influenced. I gave him that individualistic streak.

"Do you remember any of those statements? Her statements?"

"Yes. They were among the first things I ever heard."

"Please tell me."

"Okay." He frowns slightly with the effort of recall. "She's a headstrong little bitch, okay, well, so am I, she got that from me. She doesn't think she owes me anything, she doesn't think I gave her anything, it was always about her father. Well, too bad, honey, because he's dead and I'm all that's left. And now she's off with Solo, that snake in the grass, I should have known better. I did, didn't I? I knew I had to keep them separated and then like an idiot I let them meet. I will destroy that little monster, I swear, after all I've done for him, taking him in when his backstabbing, criminal parents . . . and who does Evening think cost her her father?"

I hold up my hand. "What?"

"Do you want me to repeat it? I probably missed a few words. I don't have a photographic memory. But you know that already."

"What did she say next?"

"That was it. She seemed agitated—"

"She's more or less always agitated," I interrupt.

"But then she stopped herself and said, 'You don't need to know any of that. And don't tell Evening any of it.'"

"Then why did you tell me?"

He smiles. He hasn't done that before. I gave him really good teeth. Perfect teeth. But I didn't design that smile, not exactly. That smile, that's some alchemy, some kind of magic interaction of, I don't know, but oh yes. Shiver. And warmth. And a general all-over-body feeling like I really want to cut the distance between us and it's suddenly very difficult to focus on my outrage.

I have to shake my head, hard, and replay his last statement to find my place again. "Why did you tell me if my mother said not to?"

"I'm not a machine, Evening. I'm a man. And you made me to be free. You did that, right?"

"Yes. Yes." I made him to be free? No responsibility there. Yes, I made him to be free. I wonder what else I made him to be.

That day in the lab with Aislin comes back to me in high-definition imagery. Aislin ogling, me pretending to be so much more puritanical than I really am, because that's part of my relationship with Aislin.

I see him now in memory. I see the eyeballs floating, disconnected. They look much better in his head. I see the chest I designed, the stomach I created. I picture all the choices I made.

It's disturbing.

He's here and real and beautiful and I made him beautiful. And this is why Solo would destroy my mother? Is this boy, this man, is his existence really some kind of a crime?

In what mad, unholy universe could this work of art—*my* work of art—be a crime?

My phone chimes. I hear it, but I don't really care much. Then I realize its chimed before. Several times.

"Excuse me," I say. For some reason, I feel I have to be formal with Adam. I don't know what the rules are. I've never stood around chatting with my own amazingly attractive creation before.

I fumble for my phone, my fingers not finding it in my purse. I don't want to—almost can't—take my eyes off him. I apologize again for shifting my line of sight. How dare I not gaze upon you in wonder? How dare I look down at the rat's nest that is my purse?

I find the phone. It's a message.

Maddox shot. SF General Hospital. Please come.

To my shame, I hesitate. I think, *damn him and damn her, I'm talking to Adam, here!*

But somehow, from some depth of my soul, the better side of me asserts itself and tells me I have to go.

I'll ask him to come with me.

No. No, wait, who created whom, here? I didn't create this person just to turn into the same diffident, critical, shy girl I usually am. I'm in charge in this relationship.

Right? I ask myself. Right?

"Adam," I say. "Come with me."

36

ADAM

SHE IS NOT QUITE WHAT I EXPECTED. VISUALLY, YES. VISUALLY I KNOW THAT Evening is the very epitome of young, female beauty. I know this as surely as I know anything. I have been given this truth.

But she does not quite sound as I expected her to.

She does not act precisely as I expected her to act.

I'd learned that she was headstrong, difficult, naive, very smart, very talented, with all the potential in the world.

That phrase is in my head: all the potential in the world.

That girl has all the potential in the world. She could be anything. She can do anything she wants. Anything! But she is frittering her life away hanging out with that drug addict slut loser friend of hers.

Having now spoken with Evening, I agree that she is intelligent. I don't know if she has all the potential in the world.

A thought occurs to me. "This person we are going to rescue. Is it your drug addict slut loser friend?"

We have been running down the pier toward the Embarcadero. Evening stops.

"What?" Her eyes narrow. "Where did you get that idea?" Before I can answer she interrupts with a slashing hand gesture. "Never mind. I can guess."

We run some more. We reach a trolley just as it pulls to a stop. We leap aboard, then wait impatiently for several minutes while the driver gets out and inspects his vehicle.

"Don't believe what my mother told you," Evening says.

I feel a rush of terror. "Evening, all I really know is what your mother told me. If I were actually to stop believing everything she told me . . ."

We are sitting beside each other. Her thigh and shoulder are pressed against mine. She turns to me and I turn to her and this brings our faces very close together.

"I—" she says, and then her voice makes a croaking sound. Her eyelids lower, as if she's sleepy. Slowly, slowly she's moving closer.

Suddenly, her eyes widen. I see something like alarm in her gaze as she pulls away.

"I have to sit somewhere else," she says in a rush.

"Why?"

"I just do, that's all."

She has not moved. "Where?"

"What?" Her eyes are at half-mast again. "Oh. Yes. This seat in front here."

She gets up, but just then, the trolley lurches. To keep her from falling over into the aisle I put my right arm around her abdomen and then she slips down a little so that my arm slips up and then stops because it can't go any farther.

The trolley accelerates away and centrifugal force—that's a misconception, it's actually momentum—pushes her back against me.

We are the only passengers.

She struggles a little to stand up, but her struggle is not very forceful, and she sits for a while even after the trolley has stopped decelerating.

"Oh my," she says in a strained voice.

She repeats it, but with a long pause. Like this: "Oh . . . . my." Then, sounding really as if she isn't talking to me at all but to some other person entirely, she says, "Yes, getting up. Absolutely getting up and moving. Because, no. Wrong, that's why. So. Getting up."

With a sudden heave, an uncoordinated pushing off that I find strangely enjoyable, she stands up. She looks wobbly, although the trolley is moving with admirable smoothness.

Evening drops heavily into the seat in front of me. She blows out a long sigh and runs her fingers through her hair and says—again, as though she's not really talking to me—"Okay. Okay. I can do this."

I remember her mother's words and say, "You can do anything you want."

She answers, "Mrrgghh," in a high, strained voice.

Twenty minutes later, we reach the hospital.

37

EVƎ

THE ER ENTRANCE IS A NARROW, AUTOMATIC DOOR IN A SLAB OF CONCRETE. THERE'S a cheery pink sign above that reads "Emergency Room," adorned with a blue teddy bear. I think it may be the ambulances-only entrance, but I decide I don't care. We slip in behind a gurney carrying a wildly flailing drunk.

The drunk is yelling, "Purgatory! Purgatory!", so no one notices us.

Until they notice Adam.

The gurney falters. The two guys pushing it stare, their jaws dropping a little. A woman doctor comes out, lights a cigarette, takes a puff, and stops. The smoke drifts out of her mouth. She's forgotten to exhale.

The drunk—he's an old dude, maybe sixty, maybe a hobo—stops yelling and looks baffled.

"Excuse us," I say. No one hears me. No one sees me. It's

kind of getting annoying. I do exist, after all, even when I'm standing next to Adam.

There is zero possibility that anyone will stop us as we move past the gurney and into the busy emergency room treatment area. Nurses bustle, doctors amble, everyone looks dopey-tired.

There's less shouting and drama than you see on TV shows, and the lighting is much worse. Maybe the doctors are all having interior monologues about their love lives, but it seems more likely that they're all just waiting for their shifts to be over.

Adam stops the place cold.

I'm concerned that people may be dying while the medical professionals stop to stare.

"Where's Maddox Menlow?" I ask.

Again, there is apparently no sound coming out of my mouth, so I yell, "Aislin! Where are you?"

"E.V.?"

A white curtain flies back and Aislin's head pops out of one of the treatment areas. I run to her. There's hugging. Then I look at the bed. No Maddox.

"Where is he?" I ask.

"They just took him to be operated on."

"Oh no," I say. "How bad is it?"

She has a hollowed-out look in her eyes. "They shot him in the stomach. It's . . . they don't know. I mean, there was a lot of blood."

I don't know why, but I'd just kind of assumed that if Maddox had really been shot, it was in the foot or the elbow or something. Nothing like this. Nothing potentially fatal.

I feel like a jerk.

"Was it those same guys?" I ask.

Aislin looks down at her feet, embarrassed. "Look, he didn't give them that money, the nine thousand dollars. He used it to buy some stuff. He was then going to resell it, so he could pay those guys and still keep some."

Despite vivid images in my head of a gut-shot Maddox, I can't stop the flame of anger kindling inside me. I got him that money. It wasn't so he could deal more weed.

I lean against the bed. "Did they catch the guys?"

Aislin shakes her head. "I know, all right?" Her eyes brim with tears. "I know what he is. And I finally know I have to get rid of him. But not while he's maybe dying, right?"

"Right," I say, but I don't believe she's going to dump Maddox, injured or well. She'll go back to him, like she always does. Suddenly the sheer doom of it all hits me. Aislin will spiral down with Maddox, or whatever asshole eventually replaces him.

And what's my own great plan? To help Solo destroy my mother? And then what? Wander the city homeless, with my beautiful creation in tow, stopping traffic?

I realize—and I blame Adam for distracting me—that Solo has no doubt already succeeded. The devastating data is probably on its way. My mother's doom is sealed.

Not about me, I chide myself. This is about *Aislin*.

"Let's get a cup of coffee," I say. Aislin sniffles into her sleeve, and I guide her from the emergency room to the cafeteria.

I'm sipping coffee before I realize I've left Adam behind.

"He'll be okay," I murmur.

"I don't know," Aislin says miserably, assuming I'm talking about Maddox. Then, bless her, she worries about me. "What's happening with Solo? Did you guys do it?"

For once I know that when Aislin says "do it," she doesn't mean "have sex."

"He took the flash drive and left," I say.

"Oh." She doesn't know what to say, and that's okay, because in her place I don't know that I would be thinking about anything.

Why do I love Aislin? Because with her whole life falling apart, she thinks about me. She still cares about me.

I'm not as good a friend as she is.

"So . . . your mom?" she manages.

I shrug. My stomach is churning; my head is fuzzy. I've been reacting to Adam, not even thinking. What is the matter with me? Solo's busy destroying my mother and I'm sighing over Adam.

It's just that he's so . . . perfect.

I'm so confused.

"Aislin," I say, "there's something I have to tell you. Show you. Some*one*."

"Okay. Do you have any Kleenex on you?"

I grab a couple napkins from the dispenser. "It can wait," I say. "You'll see, soon enough."

Suddenly someone sits down in one of the spare chairs. It's rude, so I shoot the interloper a chilling look.

He's a good-looking twenty-something Asian guy. He doesn't smile. He's wearing a green leather jacket. It takes a few seconds before I realize that I've seen him before. In Golden Gate Park.

The blood drains from Aislin's face.

"Get out of here, you piece of crap" she snarls.

The guy looks at her, vaguely interested and not at all intimidated. He crosses his arms on the table and leans forward.

"I don't suppose either of you ladies has a spare twelve thousand dollars, do you?"

"It's nine," I say.

"It was nine." He makes a sort of sympathetic shrug. "Interest rates are high."

"Actually," I say with all the superior condescension I can manage, "the prime rate is quite low."

It's an amazingly stupid thing to say, but he takes it in stride. "We're not the Fed. Our rates are higher."

He sees my surprise. "Yeah, I know, I'm a thug so I must be unintelligent and uneducated. Truth is, I do work with some people who are like that. But I'm three credits away from a business degree."

"Then you should be smart enough to find another job," I snap.

He laughs, but his laugh is one of those silent ones. "Yeah, if my mom was a billionaire I'd probably feel that way, too. You know what the unemployment rate is for guys my age?"

I don't. I have the feeling he does.

"I don't have any money," I say.

"Well, that's just a matter of time," he says. "Maddox had the money, didn't he? Which means he got it from you. Right? Girl-friend here doesn't have it, so it came from you." He shrugs and leans back. "Go get some more. Twelve large to Terra Spiker is like a quarter to me." He digs change out of his tight jeans, finds a quarter, holds it up between thumb and forefinger. "That's what twelve grand is to your mom."

"My mother has—" I begin.

"But you know what twelve grand is to Maddox? It's life, that's what it is. Life itself."

The strange thing is that his dark eyes aren't cold or without feeling. He seems compassionate. Almost as if he cares.

Maybe he does. Maybe he doesn't want to kill Maddox.

Answering my silent question, he says, "I hate to see things end that way. You know how I'd like things to end? You meet me tonight—I'll text you the location—and you hand me a bag with thirteen thousand dollars in it."

"It was twelve!"

"Our interest rates compound hourly. By tonight it'll be thirteen."

He starts to walk away and I yell, "You don't even have my number."

"Sure I do," he says without looking back.

Aislin doesn't say anything. She doesn't have to. The name-less guy with the quarter has taken care of that.

"How am I supposed to . . ." I begin.

"Don't," Aislin says. She puts her hand on my forearm. "You know what? Don't even. You've done more than enough. Too much. Really. This isn't your problem."

"You're my best friend. Of course it's my problem."

She looks at me gratefully, but then her gaze shifts. She rises without a word. There's a doctor in line at the cash register, holding a piece of pie.

I follow her to him.

"You're the doctor who took care of Maddox," she says, yanking on his sleeve. "What's happening?"

He looks cornered and not happy about it. "He's still in the OR. It's going to be a while. Hours."

"Hours?" I echo.

"He took two bullets. There are fragments in his spine, damage to his liver, and major internal bleeding. If he survives all that, his large intestine is perforated, which means that all kinds of bacteria have been released into his body."

"But he's going to live," Aislin says.

The doctor says, "He may."

He may?

I look at Aislin, expecting a breakdown. Her face is almost impassive. But her eyes, they tell me the truth.

The truth shocks me. It shouldn't, maybe, but it does. Her reaction to those two terrifying words, words conveying the possibility—no, the likelihood—that Maddox will die, causes a gleam.

It's gone in a heartbeat. But I know I saw it.

There's a part of Aislin that wishes Maddox would just, finally, die and free her.

Strange, maybe, but that decides it for me. I'll get the money. Because my best friend is not going to live the rest of her life feeling like she dumped her boyfriend when he was helpless.

Maddox is going to live, if I have anything to say about it.

Then she can dump the jerk.

38

SOLO

I WALK THE STREETS OF SAN FRANCISCO WITH DOOM IN MY POCKET, A HEAVY dread in my heart, and a longing to be back at Spiker delivering bagels.

Tommy will come looking for me. I'm sure of that. I knocked him off his stride, and by escaping I've probably frustrated him to the point of throwing furniture.

But he can't find me. So for now I'm safe.

Will he guess that I have the deadly information with me? Will he guess that I've hesitated to disseminate it?

What's his play? Run to Terra, no doubt. Warn her that their little creep show is over.

Why doesn't the idea of that scene make me happy? Oh, I know why: Eve. Eve has screwed everything up. Eve has messed me up. She's scrambled my brain. She's totally confused me.

Which is why I have to see her. To un-confuse myself.

Probably if I tried to re-create that kiss now it would have no effect on me. No bad effect, by which I mean no good effect, as in it would probably have no effect on me at all.

This is a confusing train of thought.

Probably I won't have a completely clear head until I test out the proposition. The one about a second kiss meaning nothing to me at all. At all.

I decide to kick a bag of trash on the sidewalk.

Anyway. Anyway. Anyway, I have to go see her, see what she's up to, see what she thinks I should do. Get her permission. Yes, her permission, no, I don't mean that. Because she is not the boss of me.

I remember when I walked in behind her and she was working on that sim—no not a sim, was it—but that's later knowledge and what I'm really remembering is the way her hair was kind of swept aside and it was with great difficulty that I did not walk over and kiss the back of her neck.

At which point, she no doubt would have turned around and punched me.

Or not.

I walk faster. It's downhill, so I can make good time. Is it possible she hasn't realized that I left with the drive? No, no way. Dammit.

Why did I?

Because I was scared. And I am never scared.

The Embarcadero is in view. Traffic is starting to pick up. The trolleys go shrieking past. There are a pair of old gay dudes walking hand-in-hand with a tiny dog on a leash. There's a street guy checking the trash for cans. There's a business chick in a gray skirt suit and sneakers. I wonder if she's the lawyer whose office I misappropriated.

I push through a mini-crowd of commuters and march purposefully toward the pier warehouse, where I will grab Eve and kiss the living hell out of her. No. First I'll ask her whether I should or should not destroy her mother and her family business.

I stop at the edge of the pier. Something is wrong. I feel it. So I stop.

And it's too late. Because there are two guys behind me, standing way too close.

"We have guns!"

I turn to look at them. It's Dr. Chen and Dr. Anapura. Big Brains. Chen is in his forties. He has a chronically startled look behind glasses he thinks make him look hip. Anapura is a woman about fifteen years older than I am. She has a long braid down her back that nearly touches her . . . well, it's really long.

"You guys absolutely do not have guns," I say.

Chen points meaningfully and nervously to a bulge beneath his jacket.

Anapura pulls something from her coat pocket that looks like a can of hair spray. It's not.

She hoses me with it, I say something brilliant like, "Hey!" and then the world goes swirly.

● ● ●

I CAN'T SAY THAT I EXPECT TO WAKE UP ANYWHERE IN PARTICULAR. BUT WHERE I do wake up is not in the pier warehouse.

The mildew smell is gone. So is the sound of water sloshing against the pilings. There's something in the taste of the air that's familiar.

I'm back at Spiker.

Strong hands grab me. There's a hood over my head. I'm being hauled up to my feet and pushed forward. They've taken my shoes. My bare feet are on carpeting. My hands are tied behind me. I sense that there are at least three or four people around me.

We go through a door.

"Wha—" I start to say, and only then does my befuddled mind realize there's a piece of duct tape over my mouth.

More doors. An elevator.

We're going down.

Out of the elevator, through a locked door—I hear them keying the combination—and then we're on another elevator. Going down again.

Going down to where? There is nothing this far down. I know the Spiker campus like I know my own face. There is no second set of elevators. There is no sub-basement.

And yet there is.

The elevator stops and I am shoved out. I stumble. I smack into something hard and unyielding, like a wall, only not. I feel it as it slides past my cheek: a steel support column.

The hood is snatched from my head.

The light is dim, ancient fluorescent cylinders way up high, hanging from unfinished concrete. We're in a large space, the size of a high school gym. Tanks of various shapes and sizes are everywhere. Tall cylinders, horizontal cylinders, giant steel-bolted aquariums.

There are objects, creatures, in many but not all of these tanks. Nearest to me, most visible, is something that must once have been a gorilla. It's been shaved, or worse yet, deliberately designed to be hairless. It looks like a wrinkled, sagging, old bodybuilder with skin the color of licorice. It's not alive, at least I hope it isn't, because it's jammed tightly into the vertical cylinder.

I count four men and one woman. Dr. Chen, Dr. Gold, Martinez, a grad student working on his PhD, and a guy named Sullivan, who works in accounting. Dr. Anapura is the only woman.

The missing person, the sixth, is standing behind me.

"Solo Plissken," Tattooed Tommy says, a regretful tone in his voice.

I size up the people facing me. Chen and Anapura are the tough ones. The rest are scared and unsure of themselves.

"Plissken?" Martinez echoes. "As in . . . ?"

"You didn't know that?" Tommy said. "You are missing out on the good gossip, dude." He moves around to a spot where I can see him. "Yes, Plissken, 'as in.' Dr. Jeffrey Plissken and his lovely wife, Isabel. As in what, three major, groundbreaking, Nobel-bait papers?"

I glare at Tommy. He rips the tape from my mouth.

"Leave my parents out of this," I say with my first breath.

"He's a gofer," Martinez protests. "He runs things through the autoclave."

Tommy looks at me, as if it's my job to explain.

"He's actually quite bright, it turns out," Tommy says. "His parents had, what, an average IQ in the 170 range? There's been some reversion to the mean, of course, so I don't believe bagel boy is quite in that league, but oh, he's smart. Aren't you, Solo?"

He leans close, cocky. He's enjoying performing for his crew. I jerk my head forward hard, a head butt.

I miss. But I make him jump back.

It's not enough to ruin his triumphant mood.

"How did you find me?" I demand.

"Well, Solo, you come with a few interesting modifications. I assume you know that you were given the same potential to heal as your little girlfriend."

Of course I know.

"She's not my girlfriend," I say. Which is a stupid and dorky thing to insist on.

"You haven't tapped that little piece yet? She's no great beauty, but she's cute enough, and she's got a nice little body."

"I'd do her," Dr. Chen says.

Dr. Anapura says, "There's no need to be sexist, Doctor."

Tommy is irritated, but he continues. "My guys weren't that far behind you. Clever, losing them in the fog, but they found where you'd docked. They caught a glimpse of you heading east on the

Embarcadero. I know the location of Austin Spiker's studio. Two plus two. Give me some credit."

"But you don't have Eve," I say.

"Mmm. Not yet. She'd been there but she's gone. For her own safety we need to find her. So tell me. Where?"

"Will it bother you very much if I say, 'screw you'?"

He grins. "Kind of expected it. It's okay. We have your flash drive. And in a few hours we'll have you doing whatever we like, including getting the girl."

"You going to beat me?"

"No. We're going to clone you. Going to make ourselves a whole new Solo. Thanks to the Plissken process, we can transfer—and edit—your memories for implantation in the clone. He'll tell us."

"The Plissken process. I'm honored."

"Oh, it's not named for you, bagel boy. It's named for the geniuses who invented it, along with the accelerated cloning process itself."

He lets it sink in. His eyes are bright with anticipation.

I blink and look away. I don't mean to.

"Yes, young Plissken, that's right. That's the truth of it. Terra Spiker? She's an A-plus businesswoman, but only a B-minus scientist. Your parents were the brains behind Spiker-Plissken Bio. As it was supposed to be known." He clucks his tongue. "Your parents would be so disappointed in you. They knew to put science ahead of anything. They knew society's restrictions are meaningless."

The others nod heartily. True believers. Acolytes.

Acolytes, not of Terra Spiker, but of my own parents.

"They also knew the profit potential of that kind of power," Tommy says. "My God, you can't even begin to imagine it. With their work—and of course the interface designed by their former grad student—we can create humans to order. Do you know what people will pay for that? I mean: O . . . M . . . G, Solo! We can create humans from scratch. We can make exact replicas. Or we can let you design your own and make it any age you want, program it any way you want. For a price, you can be God."

"And we could banish all hatred and evil and genetic disease," Dr. Chen adds.

Tommy waves a hand dismissively. "Yes, yes, save the world and all that. And make billions of dollars."

"Make the world a better place," Dr. Anapura chimes in.

"Right, whatever, let it go, would you?" Tommy says with a sigh.

I hear Tommy. I know what he's saying. But I can't move past what he's said about my own parents.

"My parents," I say, having no completion for that sentence.

"They were brilliant! They were young gods," Tommy says. "Terra found out what they were doing, that they were moving beyond mere theory, and she shut them down. She destroyed their work! She wiped their hard drives, burned their papers."

"Terra destroyed their work," I repeat.

Tommy throws his hands in the air. "It was a crime! And then of course, she sent Austin after them. And we know how that ended."

I shake my head. No. I don't know how that ended.

He's starting to tell me when Dr. Gold, who's wandered off to find something to clean his glasses with, yells from just out of sight. "Hey, Dr. Holyfield! Where's the girl's boy?"

Tommy stares at me, frozen. I stare back, just as frozen.

"What the hell are you talking about, Gold?"

Dr. Gold comes ambling back. He's not concerned, just curious. "The subject. Adam. He's not there anymore."

39

ADAM

Evening has disappeared. It takes me a while to realize this.

In the meantime, I'm getting medical attention. A doctor named Johanna has detected a possible irregularity which requires her to listen to my heartbeat. This requires me to take off my shirt. I'm sitting on a gurney with the curtains drawn around us but other doctors and nurses—Adele, Laura, Stephanie, and Steve—crowd in to assist.

"How old are you?" Dr. Adele asks.

"That depends," I answer. "Do you mean what is my apparent age? Or my actual age?"

"I just want to know if you're over the age of consent," Dr. Adele says, and the others laugh nervously. She frowns. "What is the age of consent, anyway?"

"Eighteen," someone says.

"I don't suppose you're eighteen, are you?" Dr. Stephanie says.

"Eighteen hours," I say helpfully. "Depending where you count from."

"He looks eighteen," Nurse Steve says.

The curtain slides back. It's Evening and a girl.

I have seen the girl in my memory. Her name is Aislin.

"Really?" Evening says, glaring at Dr. Adele, who lowers her stethoscope and mumbles something I can't hear.

"It's . . . oh my God, it's you." Aislin seems to be surprised in some way.

"Come on, Adam, let's go," Evening says.

"It's you," Aislin repeats.

"Yes. It is me," I say. I suspect that is close to being a joke. "I am Adam. Adam . . ."

It occurs to me that I don't know my last name. All the doctors have last names. I can see them on their name tags. Obviously, people have them, and I am people, therefore I should have one. But Terra Spiker has not put that bit of information in my head.

"Let's go!" Evening says impatiently.

But I'm frozen in place. The enormity of it. The strangeness of it. There are people all around me and each of them has a last name.

How dare they create me and not even give me a name?

"What's my last name?" I demand.

"What? Who cares?" Evening snaps. "We have to go!"

Another doctor appears. He stares at Evening. He looks down at her leg. Up at her face. She recognizes him.

"You're Evening Spiker," he says.

"Right. Um, good to, uh . . . You treated me, didn't you?"

"You're walking?"

"I am," she says.

"Unassisted."

"Yeah, I, uhhhhh. Have to go."

"I have to see the leg," he says.

"Nah, it's just a leg."

"Please. Please. Indulge me."

Evening says, "I'm shy."

"Show me the leg. Please."

Evening sighs. "I guess it doesn't matter anymore. Everything is coming out." She tries to pull up the leg of her pants, but that doesn't work, so she unbuckles her jeans and drops them to her ankles.

She has nice legs. Very athletic and shapely. But I have no idea why this man needs so badly to see them.

"Holy crap," the doctor whispers.

Evening sighs. "Show's over." She pulls her pants up. "Now, we have to go."

She grabs my hand firmly and yanks me after her.

We rush through a crowd of people in a waiting room. I see children sitting with their parents.

Do I have parents? No, I don't.

It bothers me. Even as I'm dragged along, it bothers me. I know—I've been told—that I'm different, so it's not a surprise. It's just that I'm not simply different, I'm unique.

That should be a good thing, perhaps, but it doesn't feel good.

"I want a last name," I say as we reach the outside.

"Kind of busy," Evening says, and we race to board a bus. We find seats. People gawk at me. I'm getting used to it.

"I don't like this," I say. It's true. I feel bad. I feel strange.

Aislin sits across the aisle from us. "I've always liked the last name Allbright."

"Adam Allbright?"

"My name's Aislin, by the way."

"Yes, I'm aware of your name."

She holds out her hand, very formal. She smiles. She has a nice smile. Different from Evening's. But nice. Someone has recently struck her. She has a bruise on her face, and I can see the individual fingermarks.

I shake her hand and try out the name again. "Hi, I'm Adam Allbright. Adam Allbright, nice to meet you."

Evening is looking back and forth from me to Aislin. I ask her if it's appropriate for me to call myself Allbright.

"Call yourself whatever you like."

"Adam Allbright," I say. "That's me."

40

EVƎ

AISLIN IS NOT DROOLING.

It takes me a while before I notice.

Granted, her boyfriend is in the hospital fighting for his life. But I've known Aislin for a long time. Aislin memorizes the face and form of every single attractive male who comes within sight.

Aislin doesn't look at guys and drop them into a simple binary system of "cute"/"not cute." She does detail. Amazing detail. If she can't actually see detail, she extrapolates from what she can see. Show her a guy's neck, she can draw his chest. Show her a bicep, she can tell you what his thighs are like. Show her a thigh and you really don't want to know just how much she can extrapolate.

It's her own weird genius.

Aislin is not even looking at Adam. Maybe it's overload. Maybe it's just too much for her to process. But she almost seems shy. Aislin. Shy.

I guess I'm relieved. I don't want to have to tell her to back off. Adam is mine.

According to the app on my phone, we can get off this bus and catch another bus heading back across the Golden Gate to Tiburon. It will take a while, though. Should I take a taxi?

Am I in a hurry? To get the money for Aislin, I'll have to confront my mother. Which means I'll end up telling her everything. Can I do that?

"What the hell have I gotten myself into?" I ask no one.

Adam says, "I don't know."

No, I decide. I'm not in a hurry.

I have to find my anger again. My mother used me as a biological experiment.

Yeah, and thanks to her I still have two functioning legs. Thanks to her I'll run again.

Thanks to her a lot of people dying in harsh hellholes aren't dying anymore. Or yes, they're dying, but we all die. They aren't dying today, right now, of some vile disease because my mother created Spiker Biopharm.

Instantly, all those terrifying photos come back to me. Way too high a price to pay for my leg. But was it too high a price to pay for saving countless lives? Are the two things even connected?

Couldn't my mother have done one without the other?

We get off the Muni and onto the bus for Marin County. I don't want to think anymore.

Aislin sits alone. Adam sits with me. He barely brushes against me, but that touch—two square inches of shoulder, six square inches of thigh—is charged with electricity.

"Are you sad?" he asks.

"Am I sad?" I'm going to blow him off with some facile, jokey, ironic answer. But his is not a face you joke with.

And his eyes. They're Solo's eyes—they're the same incredible blue, anyway. But there's something different about Adam's eyes. They're earnest. Utterly sincere.

"I guess I'm nervous. Or something," I say. "All my life my mother was this perfect, slightly overwhelming person. Well, you've met her."

"I don't know many people," he says. "I don't really know how to judge her."

"Then take my word for it," I say.

"Your word as my soul mate?"

So he does have a sense of humor. The sense of humor I programmed into him. Not mean. Sweet, ironic. Just the way I made him.

"Anyway, my mother," I continue, "was so high up, not even a pedestal really conveys it. It was like she lived on a cloud and I was just a regular person far down below her."

"And you also had a father?"

"I was a lot closer to my dad. He was the mid-point between me, little Evening Spiker, and the almighty Terra-Mother. We worked that way. Me to my dad to my mother. Then he died and all of that . . . Some families, maybe it would have made us closer. With us, no. My mother was still way, way up there."

"Up in the clouds."

"Figuratively. You get that, right?"

"Yes. I know that people don't live in the clouds."

Maybe that's a joke. I don't know. I turn to look at him.

We are toward the back of the bus. The seats are tall. No one can really see us. Aislin's dozing.

"What the hell am I going to do with you?" I ask Adam.

"Do you have to do something with me? It's my decision what I do with myself. Right?" He genuinely isn't sure.

I avoid answering directly. "I don't even know what I'm doing with myself. What if they actually arrest my mother? What, I live with my grandmother?"

"Do you have to live with her?"

"I don't know if I'm exactly ready for my own house," I say.

"Freedom," he says, and he gives the word surprising urgency.

"Responsibility," I counter.

"Do they go together?"

"So I've heard," I admit.

His beautiful eyes—eyes that I try not to remember as floating loose and unattached—look into my eyes. Eyes that he has never seen loose and unattached. Fortunately.

I have the advantage on him. I can remember everything about him. He can only seem to look into my soul. I can pretty much actually look into his.

"Does this mean you are responsible for me?" Adam asks.

"Do you want me to be?"

He frowns. There's an instant of panic in his eyes. It surprises me. How has he moved so quickly from childlike naïveté to existential panic?

"I don't know what I am," he says.

"You're Adam Allbright," I say, and I try to flash a smile.

"I find you beautiful, but . . ." He stops himself.

"I like the part about 'beautiful' more than whatever was going to come after 'but,'" I say lightly. Because what else am I going to do when the most beautiful boy in the world is seated beside me and several inches of him are pressed against me and I swear the taste of his breath is sweet in my mouth?

Joke.

"Do you want me to say you're beautiful?" he asks. He seems concerned.

"Who doesn't like flattery?" I ask.

"But it's not flattery. It's what I feel. I feel that you are the most beautiful—"

And that's when the bus lurches as it heads onto the Golden Gate Bridge and oh I'm even closer now and he doesn't pull away and I start to but I don't. It's not possible to pull away.

I kiss him.

He does not kiss me.

His lips are the lips I gave him.

I slip my hand beneath his arm and around his body, the body I made for him, the hard muscles I programmed him for.

Adam pulls back, gasping for air. His eyes are clouded. "I don't know what to do."

Of course, I know exactly what he should do. Biology, folks. Evolution. We're all just animals, right? Right?

Right?

I touch his chin. It's perfect. Chiseled, with a slight cleft. Sculpted-by-Michelangelo perfect.

Just the way I ordered it.

"Kissing's easy," I say, and I'm suddenly glad Aislin is asleep so she can't hear me. "Whatever you do, it'll be perfect."

We kiss.

It's just the way I ordered it.

When we come up for air, I turn to see if Aislin's still asleep.

My face burns when I realize she's wide awake and watching us.

I wait for the applause or the sarcastic, leering remark. But all she does is nod. Her smile is almost wistful.

Adam turns. He blushes, too. I must have programmed him with that gentle self-consciousness. "Hello, Aislin," he says.

"Hello," she says back.

"Lovely weather we are having," Adam says, and before you can say "what the hell is going on here?" they are having an awkward, first-date kind of chat.

I suddenly feel like a fifth wheel, so I retreat to a seat near the front. When Adam starts to follow me, I tell him to stay and talk with Aislin.

I don't know why. It just seems right.

There was something about that kiss. It was like a beautifully executed guitar riff, played without any feeling.

It was . . . not perfect.

41

SOLO

"Terra!" Tommy says.

"You think . . ." Dr. Chen says with a gasp. "You think she knows?"

"Who else would decant Adam?" Tommy rages.

"But why would she do such a thing?" Dr. Gold asks. "She doesn't even know he exists."

"Clearly she knows he exists, Doctor," Martinez says with a slight sneer on the word "doctor." "How else could she decant him?"

Dr. Anapura sees the anger in Tommy's face—mostly beneath the tattoo that says "Pixies"—and says defensively, "I checked! She hasn't been down here since the Plisskens died! And there are no cameras except the one we used to show the supposed simulation!"

"Wait a minute," I say. No one pays attention.

"Oh my God, she knows," Dr. Chen cries. He's dancing from foot to foot like a child scared of visiting the dentist.

"We'll deal with her," Tommy snarls.

"Deal with her? Deal with *her*?" Dr. Chen is nearly weeping. And I can see the fear beginning to infect the others.

Sullivan from accounting has gone pale. "I'm the one who's on the hook for moving funds around. I'm the one who has been moving money out of Level One budgets into the Adam Project." He's panting like a hunted animal. "I'm going to go to jail. I'm going to prison! What am I supposed to tell my wife?"

"I can't handle prison!" Dr. Chen wails. "I'm an intellectual!"

"Shut up, all of you," Tommy snaps. "You're scared of one middle-aged woman?"

The consensus seems to be that yes, yes they are very scared of Terra Spiker.

"Hey!" I yell. "Hey! What is this, some puppet show you're putting on for my benefit? Like Terra Spiker isn't the one behind all of this?"

Tommy turns on me, his eyes blazing. "You know, you're really not as smart as your parents, are you? Your parents? They were geniuses! Maybe when we put you in the tank we can raise your IQ a few points so you can keep up."

In the tank? I'm not sure what that means, but I can guess. Even with my limited IQ. But that's not the point. That's not why I meet Tommy's gaze and say, "Listen, Dr. Holyfield. You have to tell me."

"Yeah, so you got into my computer, good for you, kid. But you didn't learn much, did you?"

"We have to run!" Dr. Chen cries. "I have family in Guangdong Province!"

Tommy leans close, his expression cruel. "You stupid little nobody. Your parents were gods to me. Terra Spiker threatened to have them arrested. Terra Spiker forced them out of the company. You'd be worth billions, kid. Billions!"

"Why did she threaten them?" I ask, but I've already guessed.

"You think Adam was the first human we made? Before there can be perfection there has to be experimentation. The Plisskens made a baby boy. We named him Golem. He died. Because of a slight flaw in his genetic makeup."

"His sphincter was on his forehead," Dr. Anapura says.

"He didn't suffer," Dr. Gold reassures me. "He was basically stillborn."

"No," I whisper.

"It's not so easy being God," Tommy says, and a shadow passes over his face. A memory, perhaps. Or a regret. "You can't always get it right. But the Plisskens had already developed the Logan Serum. The thing that allows you to recover so quickly when I do this—"

Tommy smashes his fist into my face.

His audience gasps.

"Little Evening had a heart deformity," Tommy says. "Surgery would have been very dangerous. And the Plisskens had the cure, a side benefit of the research they were doing. Terra traded them her silence for the cure. But she tried to get them to quit. She ordered them to stop."

"You're telling me my parents were monsters?" I say. I won't show any emotion.

I can't, won't, refuse to.

But it's coming clear to me now. I don't like the picture.

It could be Tommy's lying just to mess with me. But no. The others are nodding along. They all know the story. Only I am in the dark.

I'm the fool.

"Everything you see down here, it's all their work, theirs . . . and mine. Oh, I know how your little mind works, Solo the bagel boy. I know how conventional you are. Inadequate. Thank God your parents are dead or they'd die of shame!"

My parents were monsters.

Terra Spiker is . . . I don't know quite what she is.

"Look! He's going to cry," Tommy mocks. "Dr. Anapura, Martinez, Sullivan: Get him into the tank. We'll see if we can't make him a bit more malleable."

"What about Spiker?" Dr. Gold asks.

"We're going to deal with her right now," Tommy says.

I struggle. But I'm tied up. And worse yet, I'm beaten.

I've never been beaten. Even when I box and get my ass kicked, I never lay down, I never admit defeat. But now I feel like I've been gutted. Like I've been turned inside out.

I struggle. But at some level I almost think I deserve to be shoved into the tank. I've been an idiot. I've screwed up everything.

I'm the son of monsters, and I almost destroyed Terra Spiker who . . . even now, even as they drag me away, I can't quite wrap my head around it . . . Terra Spiker, who wasn't the worst person in the world.

42

EVƎ

THE REST OF THE TRIP IS, SHALL WE SAY, AWKWARD.

I, the creator, sit by myself while my creation talks shyly with Aislin, and Aislin talks shyly with him.

I, the smart one, am feeling pretty stupid.

I'm thinking about my mother—soon to be in a federal prison. I'm thinking about the vengeful guy who dictated that fate. I'm thinking that Adam is superior to Solo in every possible way.

And I'm wishing Solo was with me.

The bus lets us out a mile from the Spiker campus. We trudge along together for a while down the steep, curving two-lane road, dodging aside to avoid being run over by the occasional BMW.

Aislin and Adam walk together. It just seems natural for me to get out in front a little.

A Porsche comes tearing around a blind corner and nearly hits Adam.

I see the driver's face. His mouth is a big O. His eyes are wide.

The brakes screech. The car stops a couple hundred yards away. The backup lights glow and the car swerves back toward us.

It stops. The window rolls down. There's a bland, vaguely familiar, middle-aged man behind the wheel. Complete mismatch between the driver and the car.

"It's him!" the man cries.

He's looking at Adam.

"Who are you?" I ask.

"Sullivan. From accounting. I—" He's confused, clutching the wheel like Wile E. Coyote holding on to his latest rocket sled. "You better look out," he says at last. "They're crazy. They're really crazy."

"Who's crazy?"

"All of them." He spits the words out. "All those scientists. They're all nuts!"

"What's happening?" I demand. I put my hands on the door, trying to convince him not to bolt. But he rears back, scared.

"I have no part in this!" he cries. "I just moved the money around. I'm not putting people in vats or, or, whatever they're planning to do."

He puts the car into gear and, with a final terrified look, goes tearing off down the road.

"We need to hurry," I say. "You two go as fast as you can. I'll run the rest of the way."

"I can run," Adam says. Of course he can run. He has amazing legs, incredible stamina, maximized lungs, all the things I gave him.

"Yeah, but Aislin doesn't so much run as trip and stagger," I point out.

Aislin makes a face that says *Yep, true.*

"Adam, take care of Aislin." I head off.

It's the first time I've run since the accident. I wasn't sure I'd ever do it again. My muscles are out of practice, but to my surprise, my breathing is smooth and easy. I wish I were in shorts, not jeans, but it still feels good. More than good.

I reach Paradise Drive and leave the cross streets and houses behind me. There's a bend in the road, with trees on one side and open hillside on the other.

Right, left, right, left. I'm in high gear now. The familiar rhythm lulls me.

Up ahead on my right is the shattered stump of a big pine tree. The small hairs on the back of my neck rise.

The stump is weathered and gray, mangled. The damage happened long ago.

Six years ago, in fact.

I know this place. I forced myself to come here once, when I was about thirteen. I touched the sharp edges of the wood. It was still clinging to life, but I knew it was dying.

Once was enough.

Now, on foot, it's unavoidable. My throat closes up and my easy breathing is a memory.

This is the place where my father died. This tree is the one his car hit when he went off the road. That drop is the slope his car plunged down.

I want to keep running, but my legs aren't having it. I slow to a walk. I stop altogether.

I bend over, hugging myself, and I sob.

No time. No time.

I gulp some air and start running again, faster than before, my legs pistoning.

• • •

FROM THE ROAD YOU CAN'T REALLY SEE THE MAIN SPIKER BUILDING, JUST THE TOP floor. I can't run down the steep driveway. I have to walk in giant going-downhill steps, fighting gravity.

I near the entrance to the underground garage. My mother's gleaming white Mercedes convertible is in her designated space. She's never put the top down.

I glance back, wondering how far behind me Adam and Aislin are. I'm scared. I've rushed in here like I have a plan.

For the first time in my life, I wish I had some kind of weapon.

I survey the garage for something weapony. My mind's racing with made-up dialogue.

Hi, Mom, Solo and I sold you out and how are you? Nice blouse. By the way, I need some more cash.

So, Mom, while you're in prison can I stay in the house alone? Please? I'm old enough!

Mom . . . what the hell?

There's a fire extinguisher near the entrance. I take it from the hook. It's surprisingly heavy. How do they expect people to use these things? But I find the size and weight and general metal-ness of the thing kind of reassuring.

Up the elevator. I have to punch in a code to get to my mother's office. For some reason, my addled brain actually remembers it.

Even now, scared, tired, and a thousand times more confused than I've ever been before in my life, even now, with some disturbing montage of Solo and Adam and Aislin and the gangbanger and the scared Mr. Sullivan from accounting, even with the eerie images from the flash drive, even with all of it swirling like a tornado inside my brain, I have energy left over to feel nervous.

Why? Because I'm going to be interrupting my mother.

My mother does not like to be interrupted.

I approach her office on tiptoe. The door to her outer office, the one inhabited by her assistants, is wide open. The computer screens are blank. The lights are low.

The portal—it's way too impressive and huge to call a door—leading to Mom's office is closed. I press my ear against it. I hear the murmur of voices. Not happy voices. Angry voices. Of course, that's normal enough in Terra Spiker's office.

My fire extinguisher bangs against a planter and instinctively I say, "Shhh!" But I doubt anyone hears. Not over the sound of yelling.

"Hey!"

I spin on my heels. A man and a woman have come up behind

me. The woman is small, dark-skinned, with penetrating eyes and an extremely long braid. The man is sweating. He is large in all dimensions and has on a name tag that reads DR. MARTINEZ.

I stare at them. They stare at me. No one knows what's going on, it seems.

"Are you here to see my mother?" I ask.

"Are you?" the woman demands.

The man asks, "Is there a fire?"

"Oh, this?" I glance down at the extinguisher in my hand. "This is—"

He leaps for me. But he's a large guy and definitely not a quick guy.

I back up, banging into the door as he slams into the wall to my right.

"Martinez!" the woman cries. "Get her!"

"Get me?" I repeat it in shock. Seriously? *Get her?* It sounds so comic book.

"She's the boss's daughter," Martinez protests.

"We're probably going to kill the boss," the woman points out in a voice that's all reasonableness, with just a tinge of hysteria.

This isn't news to Martinez, but he seems embarrassed by it. It's something they don't want to say in front of me.

Martinez lunges. I push back against the door. It gives way and I stumble back. I drop the extinguisher. It rolls a bit, then comes to a stop. I catch myself before I can fall, then pivot to see the tableau before me.

My mother's office is as extreme as ever. The waterfall still pours. My father's extraordinary, oversized sculptures still hang on wires from the impossibly distant ceiling.

My mother stands behind her desk. She is casually dressed in a custom suit flown in from her London designer, a twenty-thousand-dollar watch, and a diamond necklace worth more than the lifetime wages of a hundred Guatemalan families combined. As always, she radiates the scent of Bulgari. I can't see her shoes, but I am morally certain that they are *not* a beat-up pair of Nikes.

"Evening," she says, frosty as ever. "Your timing is unfortunate."

Tommy, the scientist with the tattoos, is here. There's also an Asian guy and a shrimpy little middle-aged nerd.

Tommy has a gun in his hand. No one else is armed, as far as I can tell. The gun holds my attention. It's funny how a gun will do that, kind of make everything else blur into the background while the gun occupies the entire foreground.

I'm suddenly feeling a certain sympathy for Maddox. It must have been terrifying, seeing that gun leveled at you. Watching the trigger being squeezed.

I remember that Aislin and Adam aren't that far behind me. But neither of them has a gun. They won't help. They'll just make things worse.

Where is Solo? Sullivan said something about vats.

I'm trembling.

Is Solo dead?

"Tommy, Tommy, Tommy," my mother says, with a condescension that would shrivel a medieval baron, "you do realize you're not going to manage this, don't you?"

"I've managed it so far, bitch," he says. Even he seems appalled by the B-word. The temperature in the room drops ten degrees. No one breathes.

"I made a mistake trusting you," my mother says regretfully.

"I made a mistake thinking you were a scientist," Tommy snaps.

"There's a difference between Gregor Mendel and Doctor Frankenstein," my mother says.

"Oh, of course," Tommy sneers. "Go straight to Frankenstein. Your analogy is as feeble as your commitment to science."

"Science is learning, Dr. Holyfield," my mother says. "What you are doing is not about learning. It's about money and power."

"Aren't you going to trot out the old chestnut about 'playing God'?" Tommy asks.

He's handling the gun casually, waving it as he gestures. Getting his nerve up. He's arguing because he doesn't yet have the nerve to shoot.

No. No.

I don't want my mother to be shot. I don't want anyone to hurt her.

I love her.

She may even love me.

And damn, is she cool. No wonder Tommy can't pull the trigger. My mother is untouchable. She's as cold and perfect—and yet beautiful—as one of my father's sculptures.

My mother listens carefully to Tommy's question. She nods, as if considering. Slowly, deliberately, she walks around the desk. She comes into full view and I win my little bet with myself: Her shoes are Prada.

She steps up to Tommy. They're about the same height, but somehow my mother manages to seem like she's a foot taller. Tommy waves the gun, but he's not ready to shoot her. And he has to visibly restrain himself from stepping backward.

"You ridiculous, inadequate little man," she says. "You want to know about playing God? I've played the part. Let me tell you about it. I had a daughter. She was near death. And I had the cure. I could wave my hand . . . well, inject a virus carrying a DNA modification . . . and I knew she would live. My husband and I—" Her voice cracks, but so minutely I doubt anyone else notices. "My husband and I asked ourselves whether it was right. Whether we could 'play God' and save her life with a treatment we knew was untested. A treatment that couldn't be tested, yet, because I had broken some rules finding it."

"Great autobiogra—" Tommy starts to say.

"Shut up," my mother says. And he shuts up.

I'm looking at the fire extinguisher. I'm looking at my father's sculptures. There's the towering redwood tree reaching toward the ceiling. Near it, something that is most likely a hawk, but almost unrecognizable except as a dramatic expression of speed and rapacity, hovers overhead, its beak twelve feet off the ground.

And just three feet away from that soaring beak is the gleaming steel and Plexiglas thunderbolt.

The end of the thunderbolt is pointed in a particularly vengeful-looking way at my mother's head. Of course, if her head were to move, it would be pointed at Tommy's head.

"So I used the treatment," my mother continues. "And my partners"—she gives that word a cruel twist—"said okay, let us use it on our son as well. He was perfectly healthy, mind you. But they said, if you don't, well, we'll go public and destroy you. So I gave in. They thought they had me." She manages a tight smile. "And I guess they did. I tolerated their blackmail. Which isn't very God-like, is it?"

"They were doing science," the little short guy blurts out.

"Oh, they were brilliant," my mother allows. "Brilliant. And when they came up with a green pig I let it go, because they were on their way to great discoveries. But the more they worked, the more I began to wonder if maybe they were a little less brilliant than they thought they were." She hesitates. "Then they created that sad abomination of a child. And I realized that's what my God-playing had wrought."

"Aww," Tommy drawls. "Did the little mutant make you queasy? All your moral qualms didn't stop you from decanting your daughter's little science project, did they?"

"I had to do it," my mother says. "He was a living human being, fully formed, capable of feeling."

"Capable of luring your daughter back," Tommy counters.

"That, too," my mother concedes.

"Spare me. In the end, this whole thing made you rich."

"No. It cost me a fortune, actually. No, Dr. Holyfield, I got rich off a simple patent for accelerating the production of flu vaccines. Every time a dose of flu vaccine is made, I get twenty-one cents. A billion doses a year, that adds up to real money."

I bark out a laugh. I don't know why.

"There's no patent under your name," the woman with the braid says.

"No. It's under my husband's name. It's funny. I gave it to him as a birthday gift I don't think he really appreciated it." She sounds a little wistful. "Maybe it's because I described it by its patent number. I don't think he ever looked it up."

My mother smiles, a smile meant just for me. "He was an artist, you know. They don't think like scientists. Fortunately, we had a daughter who's always had the ability to think like both."

Sweet lord. I practically burst into tears.

Tommy's face hardens. He doesn't like the reference to me. It makes him nervous. He extends his arm. The gun is pointed straight at my mother's chest.

"Leave her alone," I say.

"You stupid little nobody," Tommy says to me. "Don't you know she killed your father?"

I shoot a wild look at my mother.

She winces.

"It's true. More playing God," my mother says.

"Mom!" It's a sob torn from my throat.

"I sent him after the Plisskens," she says. For the first time in, like, forever, she touches me. It's her hand on my hand. I don't pull away.

"I said something stupid to him. I said, 'Austin, you have to stop them. No matter what.'"

Tommy is laughing to himself. He's enjoying this part.

"Your dumbass father took it literally," he says. "And they talk about scientists not getting human nuance."

"I wasn't sure what they would do," my mother says. "I'd just expelled them from the company. I told them I was going to have them arrested. They were unbalanced. Like this tattooed buffoon here." She flips a manicured hand at Tommy. "Mentally unbalanced. I was worried for their son. I sent your father after them. Rainy night . . . and you've seen the road. He caught up with them and there was a terrible accident. Both cars went down the incline. I was just behind them with security. . . . There was a horrible fire. They were all dead when I got there."

"Listen," I say, and again my voice betrays me by wobbling. "I helped Solo. He sent everything out. All the documentation on Adam. All the rest."

My mother is not surprised. "I thought it might be something like that. Well, if that's the case, Dr. Holyfield, you and your little band of mediocrities are wasting your time, aren't you?"

"We don't have any proof he sent anything," Tommy says. "And as of a few minutes ago, nothing had hit the Internet."

I'm in the difficult position of hoping for two opposite things at once. If Solo has sent the information out and Tommy realizes it, he'll have no reason to do anything worse: The jig will be up.

On the other hand, my mother will probably be arrested along with Tommy.

And why hasn't the information been sent? Where *is* Solo?

"We have to make this look like suicide," Tommy says thoughtfully. He scans the office, snaps his fingers. "Murder-suicide! She has to kill the girl and then herself."

"Why, exactly, would I be doing that?" my mother asks.

Tommy's cronies all look troubled and thoughtful. But no one is exactly objecting.

"You fought," Tommy says. "Everyone knows your daughter hates you."

"That's not true!" I cry.

"She's found out the truth." Tommy grins. "About how you used her as a lab rat for the healing gene." He's pleased with his solution. He narrows his eyes at my mother. "And speaking of finding out the truth, how is it you found out about our . . . efforts?"

She responds with a slight smile. "You're not the only one with secret surveillance cameras, Thomas."

Tommy looks a bit deflated. "Grab the girl."

Dr. Gold and Martinez lunge for me.

I slip down, almost like I'm fainting. Martinez's arms grapple with Dr. Gold's as I slither out beneath them. I make a wild grab for the fire extinguisher. I fumble it, it's too heavy, but it trips Martinez.

He lands hard against the desk. I'm still trying to grab my only weapon. I can't get the handle, but I can get my hands around the middle of the thing and with a desperate effort I slam it back.

I aim at Dr. Gold's midsection. It misses but hits his knee.

"Ahhhh! Ahhhh! Hey, that hurt! Oh, that hurts!"

"Sorry," I say. Because I'm not really thinking clearly. Then I get a better purchase on the extinguisher and swing it wildly.

It misses, unbalancing me, and I plow forward.

"Just get her, you idiots," Tommy yells. "Anapura, help!"

"That's *Dr.* Anapura!" she snaps. She grabs for me.

I know it's a silly cliche to suggest that all scientists are nerds or dorks. But if this was a group of, say, football players, I'd be so dead by now.

"What the hell!" It's Aislin.

Her cry distracts everyone, and I slip past Dr. Anapura. I drop the extinguisher because it's just slowing me down and I know what I have to do now.

I catch sight of Adam out of the corner of my eye. He's looking to Aislin for instructions. Aislin, bless her crazy heart, reaches out with one hand, snatching Tommy's hair and yanking it like she's planning on stuffing a pillow.

"Dammit!" Tommy cries.

I climb the sculpted redwood. It isn't easy. You'd think something made of steel bands interlaced like some overly ornate Eiffel Tower would be easy to climb, but no, I'm slipping and my knees are skinned and I'm only helped by the fact that Anapura and Martinez are baffled by my move. And by the fact that Dr. Gold is acting like a scared monkey, clutching his injured knee while he howls and hops in a circle of pain.

I scrabble up and Aislin yells, "Look out!"

Just in time, I realize I'm about to jam my head into one of the "branches."

It's high up here, really high.

But it's nothing like the height Solo and I rappelled together.

"Get that guy!" Aislin orders Adam.

But Adam, I notice with a sort of distant awareness, is frozen.

Oh. Courage. I gave him everything else. I guess I forgot that.

Tommy has had enough of the chaos. He pushes the barrel of the gun into my mother's chest, and I know what she's thinking: huge dry-cleaning bill.

"Die, you cold bitch," Tommy says.

Adam shrinks back, but Aislin yells, "Get your hands off the cold bitch, asshole."

I reach the uppermost part of the steel redwood. I turn, my ankle twists, and I half-fall, half-leap onto the fat end of the thunderbolt.

"Mom!" I cry.

The lightning bolt swings forward. The point will hit my mother right in the back of her head.

The jagged point arcs forward. Inches from spearing the back of my mother's head, right through her carefully coiffed hair.

At the last possible second, she simply tilts her head to the side.

The bolt shoots past her and stops.

It stops when the point enters Tommy's forehead, just beneath the Pixies tattoo.

Great band. But not armor.

Tommy drops like a sack of rocks. The gun skitters across the floor.

Adam bends and picks it up. He considers it for a moment, then hands it to Aislin.

The rest of Tommy's gang is about to rush her when Aislin levels the gun and says, "There's a reason he handed *me* the gun. I will totally shoot you."

I swing back and forth on the thunderbolt for a while. I don't much like the idea of dropping while it's still moving. I've had enough trouble with leg injuries lately.

My mother—who has not broken a sweat, or even so much as caused a hair to move out of its assigned place—snaps her fingers at Adam. "Get her down."

Adam does. I slide to the ground along the length of his perfect body and come to rest with my mouth just inches from his perfect mouth.

He's perfect.

"Solo," I say. "We need to find Solo."

43

EVƎ

WHILE THE SECURITY GUARDS HANDCUFF TOMMY'S GROUP, I GLANCE AT HIS BODY sprawled on the floor.

I saw a bit of gore when I was at the hospital, so I'm a little less squeamish than I used to be. Still, seeing brains on the floor isn't easy.

Adam takes one look and practically swoons. Aislin holds him up and gives me a look.

"Yeah, well, I didn't focus on physical bravery all that much," I admit. "But he'll be kind and nice and gentle."

"Could be worse," Aislin says.

"We still need to deal with the Maddox mess," I say.

"I'm going to need this carpet replaced," my mother mutters. "Kashmir silk, hand-knotted. What a waste."

"Maybe now's not the best time," Aislin whispers.

"First things first: Solo," I say.

"I know where they must have him," my mother says.

She leads the way—because she always leads the way—and Aislin and Adam and I fall into step behind her.

The room is dark. My mother flicks several switches, and there he is, floating in the tank Adam had once occupied.

"Solo," I whisper.

He's fully clothed, obviously unconscious, tangled in a web of wires.

My mother checks a glowing monitor.

"The readouts show heartbeat and brain activity all normal," she reports. "He's alive. We can decant him."

"Thank God," I say.

"I used to live here," Adam tells Aislin in a chirpy voice.

She pats his arm. "I know, sweetie."

My mother has her hand on a lever. "You know, Evening," she says, a gleam in her eye, "this would be an opportunity to . . . tweak."

Aislin rubs her palms together. "He's all hooked up. You could make some minor changes. Right?"

"Psychological," my mother suggests.

"Physical," Aislin says. "You know. In the name of science and all."

"With just a few hours and a few adjustments, you could make him more agreeable," my mother points out. "Men can be so . . . uncooperative."

I shake my head. "Let's get him out. Now."

"Last chance," my mother offers. "You know how picky you can be."

"Now."

It takes an hour to get Solo out and detached. He doesn't wake up until we have him returned to his room. He's covered in a clear viscous goo from the vat.

I place a blanket over him, just as his quite beautiful eyes flutter open.

"I'm alive," he observes.

"Yes. You seem to be," I say.

His eyes go to my mother and they widen in fear. Then he looks away. "Damn."

"Yes," my mother says dryly. "I'm still here."

"Not what I meant," he says in a subdued voice. "I . . ."

"You set out to destroy me," Mom says.

"I didn't," he says simply. "I was ready to. I could have."

I say, "Why didn't you?"

He shrugs. "It wasn't just her and me anymore. It was you, too. I could take her down. Not you."

"Sweet," my mother says in the voice she uses when she wants to make you hide in a corner.

"Tommy told me about my folks," Solo says. "I didn't know all that. I didn't know what they did, who they were. I thought . . . well, I thought you were just a ruthless, amoral, manipulative, cold bitch."

Mom nods. "Yes. All that's true."

"Okay, then," Solo says uncertainly.

Poor Solo. I think he's half-expecting one of those heart-warming TV moments. Wrong crowd for that.

Solo looks over at Aislin. He smiles.

Then he notices Adam.

"Oh my God." Solo blinks. "It's you."

"I am Adam," Adam says. "Adam Allbright."

Solo turns his gaze to me. "So. Your perfect guy."

I shrug. "Yeah, well, perfect isn't quite right for me."

"Seriously?" He's incredulous. He looks over at Adam again. "I mean, damn, Eve. Dude is amazing."

"I'm going for slightly less than amazing."

I am trying desperately to be as romantic as I can be with my mother in the room. Solo is, of course, screwing it up.

"But look at him!" Solo urges. "I'm totally straight and I'd do him."

"Thanks," Adam says.

"You want me over him?" Solo asks. "Are you nuts?"

"Apparently," I say.

"I am too perfect for Evening," Adam volunteers. "But that's all right." He smiles shyly at Aislin. "I am not too perfect for Aislin."

Solo struggles to sit up. He's woozy. I join him on the bed and help him sit up. This involves putting an arm around his back. I brush his damp hair out of his eyes.

His back isn't as nice as Adam's. His hair isn't as nice, either.

But I remember kissing Adam. And I remember kissing Solo. And I know which one I want to do again.

Well, okay, both. But more Solo.

Solo gazes at me. He has amazing eyes. The same heart-stopping blue as Adam's.

But there's something in Solo's eyes that I just couldn't find in Adam's.

"Would it be okay if I tried sketching you sometime soon?" I ask.

"Would it be okay if I tried kissing you sometime soon?" Solo asks.

"You're all covered with that goo medium from the vat," I point out. "You need a shower."

"Good point." Solo traces an index finger along my wrist.

I glance over my shoulder and realize that my mother, Adam, and Aislin have all slipped out of the room.

We're alone.

"I can get you to the shower. After that you're on your own," I say.

He takes one weak hand and wipes the goo from it on my hair. "Now you need a shower, too." He tries out a suggestive look.

"Oh please: You're weak as a kitten," I say.

He kisses me and I kiss him back, goo and all. Then I remember that Solo recovers very quickly.

So I walk him to the shower.

ACKNOWLEDGMENTS

Many thanks to the dedicated, talented, and just generally amazing people who helped create E V Ǝ & A ᗡ A M : Holly West, assistant editor; Rich Deas, art director; Ashley Halsey, interior designer; Dave Barrett, managing editor; and Nicole Moulaison, production manager.

Special thanks to Jean Feiwel, who came up with the concept and agreed in advance to cover post-collaboration marital counseling.

SQUARE FISH

EVE & ADAM
by Michael Grant and Katherine
Applegate

1. Eve's mother asks her to create the perfect boy. What characteristics would you give the perfect boy or girl?

2. Aislin's boyfriend is a drug dealer, and when he gets in trouble, she goes to Eve for help. What would you have done in Eve's place? In Aislin's?

3. Solo has worked for years to expose Terra, but now that he has proof, revealing it could hurt Eve, whom he likes. Do you agree with the choices he makes?

4. *Eve & Adam* was originally inspired by the story of Adam and Eve from the Bible. Can you find the similarities? What do you think about the changes the authors made?

5. Eve's viewpoint was written by Katherine Applegate, while Solo's chapters were written by her husband, Michael Grant. How do you think this dual perspective affected the story? Is it stronger with the two different viewpoints? Could this story have been told from just one perspective?

GOFISH

QUESTIONS FOR THE AUTHORS

**Katherine Applegate and
Michael Grant**

**What did you want to be
when you grew up?**
KA: A vet.

MG: James Bond.

KA: But we've accepted the fact that we're never going to grow up.

What's your favorite childhood memory?
MG: The best part of childhood is childhood's end.

KA: I was not actually a big fan of childhood. I like to control my life.

What was your favorite thing about school?
MG: I did not like anything about school. Not a single thing.

KA: I liked the girls' room because that's where I would hide to avoid school.

**What was your first job, and what was your
"worst" job?**
MG: Toys 'R' Us—I had to get a fake ID to work at age sixteen. I was a stock clerk.

KA: I waited tables at a place where there was no privacy, not even to change into my uniform. THAT wasn't great.

MG: We agree on our worst job, it was our last job before we were first published. We were cleaning toilets for a living.

KA: Mmm. Not fun.

How did you celebrate publishing your first book?
KA: Quitting the aforementioned cleaning gig.

Where do you write your books?
KA: I seem to need a new location for each book. At the moment, I have a desk in the living room, as close to the deck doors as I can get.

MG: I really like to work outside. So if weather allows, I work on our upstairs deck.

What sparked your imagination for *Eve & Adam*?
MG: Girl creates boy. That's the meat of it. That was the coolness from our point of view.

If you could change one genetic trait in yourself, would you? What would you change?
KA: I have weak ankles. As a result, I was not able to pursue an athletic career. Well, that plus I have no athletic talent.

MG: I would change my tendency to put on weight. It's a lifelong struggle. And it's so boring losing weight.

What is your favorite kind of new technology?
MG: I want Google Glass. I'll look like a huge dork, but I don't care.

KA: I have a milk foamer. Okay, that's not exactly cutting-edge technology. But I like it for coffee.

Who do you relate to more, Evening or Solo?
KA: Actually, we both like Solo. He's a little weird. We're a little weird.

What makes you laugh out loud?
KA: The movie *Airplane!*

MG: Ditto. Also *The Book of Mormon*, the Broadway show. That is my first-ever Broadway name-check.

What do you do on a rainy day?
MG: We both get depressed. Neither of us can stand overcast days.

If you were stranded on a desert island, who would you want for company?
MG: Katherine, of course.

KA: He is so well-trained. I'd like a slightly younger Sean Connery.

MG: Oh, well, if we're going that way, then I'd want Sofia Vergara. Take that.

If you could travel anywhere in the world, where would you go and what would you do?
KA: I'd like to go back to China. We adopted our daughter from China.

MG: Yeah, and I missed out on that trip since I stayed with our son. But, absolutely China, Japan, I've never been to the Far East.

What do you consider to be your greatest accomplishment?

MG: Well, we've been together for thirty-four years. I know that will make people roll their eyes, but that's the biggest.

KA: Then, the kids.

MG: Then, our careers.

ABOUT THE AUTHORS

KATHERINE APPLEGATE is the author of many books for children and young adults, including the Newbery Medal–winning *The One and Only Ivan*, and the award-winning *Home of the Brave*. You can visit Katherine on the Web at katherineapplegate.com.

MICHAEL GRANT is the author of the BZRK series and the bestselling Gone series. Together as "K.A. Applegate," he and Katherine wrote the very popular Animorphs series. *Eve & Adam* is their first credited collaboration. Katherine and Michael live in Northern California with their two children and numerous unmanageable pets. You can visit Michael on the Web at themichaelgrant.com.